Praise for

THE HOUSE OF BRADBURY

"Readers will find magic in *The House of Bradbury*, which weaves a contemporary Hollywood storyline with authentic Los Angeles literary history. The effect is a sparkling premise, memorable characters, and crisp dialogue that draws in the reader. Author Nicole Meier whips up a thoroughly enjoyable modern story of self-discovery."

—LIAN DOLAN,
creator and host of Satellite Sisters, author of bestselling novels *Helen of Pasadena* and *Elizabeth the First Wife*

"Just as inspiration hits struggling writer Mia Gladwell, she agrees to take in a recovering young starlet. With Ray Bradbury's former home as its backdrop, Nicole Meier weaves a delightful tale of accidental friendships and second chances."

—AMY SUE NATHAN,
author of *The Good Neighbor* and *The Glass Wives*

"In her charming, wry debut, Nicole Meier brings together a frustrated writer, a Hollywood ingénue, and the weathered home of a literary great. Through a winsome protagonist and a perfectly painted Los Angeles backdrop, Meier reminds us that although we're built on history, a wide open path still lies ahead."

—MICHELLE GABLE, international bestselling author of *A Paris Apartment* and *I'll See You in Paris*

"*The House of Bradbury* is a thoughtful and witty book about picking yourself up when life is unfolding in an unexpected and challenging way. Nicole Meier skillfully illustrates that opening up to new experiences can be richly rewarding—and surprising. As a Southern California resident and fan of literature, I was delighted by the way Meier creatively weaves her fictional story into the history of the Bradbury home."

—LISA HENTHORN, author of *25 Sense* and television writer of *Swingtown, The Beautiful Life,* and *The Glades*

The

House

of

Bradbury

The House of Bradbury

by

Nicole Meier

Published by SparkPress, a BookSparks imprint,
A division of SparkPoint Studio, LLC
Tempe, Arizona, USA, 85281
www.gosparkpress.com

Published 2016
Printed in the United States of America
ISBN: 978-1-940716-38-1 (pbk)
ISBN: 78-1-940716-39-8 (e-bk)

Library of Congress Control Number: 2015956246

Cover design © Julie Metz, Ltd./metzdesign.com
Cover photo: Palm trees courtesy Shutterstock;
drawing of house by Windy Waite
Author photo © Justin Earl Photography
Formatting by Stacey Aaronson

*Everyone must leave something behind when he dies,
my grandfather said. A child or a book or a painting or a
house or a wall built or a pair of shoes made.
Or a garden planted.
Something your hand touched some way so your soul has
somewhere to go when you die, and when people look at
that tree or that flower you planted, you're there.*

—RAY BRADBURY, *Fahrenheit 451*

CONTENTS

ONE

⌣

*M*ia stood outside the house and exhaled. Something about this moment called for deep breathing, a cleansing. Her arms felt as if they would collapse from the weight of the overfilled packing box, and its jagged corners were poking into her ribs. She needed to set it down, but her feet remained rooted. This was it. Time to walk through the door and begin the rest of her life. If only she could move.

"It's so *yellow*," Emma said, scowling at the house as she made her way along the narrow, buckled sidewalk. She stood beside her younger sister and gawked.

"It's supposed to remind you of sunshine," Mia said, feeling her cheeks flush.

"Well, it reminds me of something, all right. You're going to have to invest in some paint." Emma reached around and relieved Mia of her load. "Go on," Emma nudged her. "Take the key out and unlock your new house." With one more inhale, Mia climbed the stone steps, gripping the chipped white railing. With the turn of a worn key, she stepped inside.

"Why you would want to live in some dead writer's house is beyond me," Emma huffed, plunking down the moving box at her feet. The women lingered in the front hall, gazing at the void. Mia wrapped her arms around herself, barely able to contain her joy. Emma's arms were also locked into a tight fold as she eyed her surroundings, afraid to touch anything for fear of getting dirty. The two remained silent for a long moment. Little beams of light poked their way through slits in the window coverings. Loose particles of dust danced in the air like glitter, giving the front room a mystical feel.

As she brushed her long chestnut bangs aside, Mia's eyes drifted to the wide rafters of the tall, arched ceiling. Her skin tingled. She couldn't believe her good fortune. It was like being given a private pass into a museum and granted permission to reach out and touch every treasured surface. "Because it's Ray Bradbury's house, that's why," she said, as if that was explanation enough. Emma starred quizzically at her sister.

"You don't get it, but I do. This house has history. This house has a story. All kinds of important works were created here." As Mia spoke she crossed the wood floor to run her hand along a lean, ivory-colored mantel, trailing a finger across the intricate molding. A welling of sentiment lodged firmly in her throat. Breathing in the faint leathery perfume of aged books, she rubbed a layer of fine dust between her forefinger and thumb and thought about what it took to arrive at this moment.

At thirty-eight years old, she had finally purchased her

first house. Her own house, yes, but more than that, a house that for the past fifty years belonged to Ray Bradbury, science fiction and fantasy writer, poet, and literary genius. He was someone who was driven by his love of books. He had seemed to care about stories more than any author she'd come across, and that's what Mia found most endearing.

When she'd first read the *LA Times* article announcing that the esteemed author's house was up for sale, wonky bookshelves, ancient kitchen, claustrophobic basement, and all, Mia wanted nothing more than to get inside that house. She pored over every detail of the real estate section, hoping to glean some kind of secret about the late author's home located in the historic Cheviot Hills neighborhood where the likes of Lucille Ball, Stan Laurel, and other Hollywood greats once resided. Without thinking, she'd jotted down the west Los Angeles address and eagerly hopped in her green hatchback to seek it out.

Two months and $1.5 million later, Mia Gladwell was the proud owner of that very house, warts and all. She was charmed by its rough edges and timeworn finishes, because they represented well-loved imperfection. This quality was what made the place feel real, unlike all the other pink stucco cookie-cutter developments that were suffocating the Southern California landscape. And while the price was ridiculously beyond her freelance writer's budget and the property needed a lot of care (a full gut job, according to her sister), Mia felt like she'd landed a bargain.

When the realtor first let her inside, Mia's hair practically stood on end. She'd felt jittery and dizzy, like she was meeting a celebrity for the first time. She was sure Bradbury's creative spirit had seeped into every nook and cranny of the split-level home. From the dark old floorboards to the much-utilized kitchen cupboards, Mia could envision Bradbury making his way from room to room, pulling beloved hardbacks from the bookshelves and retrieving a favorite snack from the refrigerator, with its well-worn handle. There had been so much grime in the grout of the blue-tiled counters, she wasn't sure if anyone had bothered to take a cleaning spray to any of it. But none of this mattered to her; she recognized the home's magic and felt a strong connection right away. On a high from her initial house tour, she'd sped across town to her ex's office and convinced him to lend her a substantial sum of money to be paid back at a much later date.

As if she was reading Mia's thoughts, Emma wondered out loud, "I still don't understand how you felt okay borrowing money from Carson. You'll be forever tied to him now."

Carson Cole was not only Mia's ex-fiancé, and dirtbag extraordinaire, according to Mia's family, but he was also one of the West Coast's most successful movie producers with an absurd amount of cash, which he usually didn't know what to do with. After three years of courtship, one hefty engagement ring given then taken back, and multiple not-so-discreet affairs with young Hollywood starlets, Mia convinced her ex that he owed her.

"We have an agreement," Mia said, doing her best to avoid eye contact. "He gets why this house is important to me. Not everyone has to understand."

"And what else does he get in return?" Emma could be

like a pit bull sometimes, grabbing hold of something with her teeth, unwilling to let it go. "By partnering up with him, you've committed yourself to something and you don't even know what it is!"

Mia shooed the air with her hand and moved past the reproach. She had no interest in engaging in yet another argument with her sister regarding the topic of Carson. But Emma's concern gnawed on the edge of Mia's mind nonetheless. Initially, she'd dismissed the question of just what her ex was expecting in return for his generosity. She'd been too caught up in the euphoria of the house-buying frenzy to give it any levelheaded thought.

But now that the deal was done, the proposition was proving difficult to ignore, especially since a cascade of Carson's missed calls were currently filling up the screen of Mia's cell phone like tiny red alerts.

Determined to keep busy and postpone the blinking messages, Mia shook her head and made her way through the formal dining room and into the kitchen. Flipping yellowing light switches as she went, she noted Emma scurrying behind. It grated on her nerves to hear her sister audibly clucking her tongue like a nervous hen, calculating how much cleaning product it was going to take to rid the house of its previous tenants.

"Oh dear," Emma sighed. "When, exactly, are you going to remodel this kitchen?" Emma had a point maybe; the finishings looked their age. The robin's egg blue countertops had seen better days, and the appliances appeared as if they were on their last legs. Brown and navy flowers danced along the wallpapered room, giving it an old-fashioned but cheery feeling. A discolored louvered corner window let in the midday light. There wasn't a dishwasher, and the cabinets were mismatched. The floor in the breakfast nook and kitchen featured a prominent floral-patterned tile that complemented the wallpaper. It was as if the house had been frozen in time since the 1970s, or even earlier, to when the Bradburys purchased the home in 1958.

To Mia, all of these nuances were like a roadmap of the Bradbury family's daily life. Placing her palm over a cabinet knob, she closed her eyes and envisioned a family getting out their breakfast and starting their day together. She imagined someone making tea, someone making toast. It felt homey and pleasant and the opposite of lonely.

"Listen, I know you're Martha Stewart's clone and all." Mia turned toward her sister. "But I'm going to need you to stop bashing my new house and be supportive. I bought this place for a reason and I happen to like everything that comes along with it." Emma opened her mouth, her lacquered lips a perfect pink shimmer, but nothing came out. If she were at a loss for words, it would be a first.

Detecting commotion from somewhere outside, Mia jerked her head. "Let's go. I think I hear the moving truck pulling up." She jogged out the front door without waiting for Emma to follow.

Outside, she found her only brother-in-law climbing out of his 1982 rust-colored Volvo wagon. Tom Hutter was the only person Mia knew who still drove a diesel engine. Tom liked things old-school. He liked his bad Sanka coffee, which he always drank from the same mug, his chinos that frayed at the cuff, and his rickety old car, but most of all he loved Mia's sister.

"You came!" Mia wrapped him in a tight hug. He smelled of rye bread and coffee. She linked her arm through his and excitedly led him up to the house.

"So this is the famous Ray Bradbury's house," Tom said, as they crossed the front path. Mia knew that since Tom was a devoted history professor he could appreciate the old estate. "Wow, this is cool." He opened his arms to their full span, gesturing to the space around him. "Congratulations, kid." He met Mia's gaze with an approving nod. Mia never had a brother, but she imagined this is what it would feel like. When she was small, she used to wish for a brother. She dreamed of having someone to tromp around with and build forts, someone who would always have her back, no matter what. She craved a sibling who would not boss her around like Emma did, but would encourage her to be bold and brave. To have Tom's endorsement meant a great deal to her.

Just then a shriek came from inside. "Emma?" They both hurried through the foyer.

"There are bookshelves in the shower!" She hollered from one of the bathrooms as if she had just discovered a dead rat. "And they are built-in!"

Mia shook her barely brushed brown hair and let a giggle escape. "Wait till she finds the blue toilet." Tom gave an enthusiastic thumbs-up.

Mia admired the late author for his passionate devotion to literature. Who else would forgo shower space to make room for so many books? But not everyone agreed. Clearly, the lack of function was too much for Emma Hutter's Container Store sensibilities. She was probably stretching out a measuring tape in the bathroom at that very moment and checking her smartphone for how quickly she could schedule a contractor.

"I gotta go see!" Tom bounded up the half flight of stairs, his loafers making soft thuds on the hardwood as he went. Mia sat down on the bottom step and listened to their muffled mumbling echo through the walls. Balancing her elbows on her bare knees, she soaked in the reality of her new home. Everything had a stuffy oak smell like a neglected old attic that's been flung open for spring-cleaning. Lazy golden sunlight streamed in through the wooden shutters, and a muted hum of cars could be heard just beyond the front door. Everything felt peaceful and welcoming, like a warm hug. Mia looked upward and mouthed a *thank you* to the universe.

TWO

⌒

*H*unched down in the dining room, Mia began tackling the sea of color-coded boxes that (thanks to Emma) were stacked assembly-line-style along the wainscoted wall. She'd unpacked the essentials the previous day, but until now, the amount of belongings she had accumulated over the years had been collecting dust in the back of Emma and Tom's garage. There were Pottery Barn breakfast dishes and towel sets from her cohabitating days with Carson, a bread-making machine (*Why?*), workout equipment (another *Why?*), and her volumes of timeless literature that she no longer read but couldn't possibly give away.

Thanks to Ray Bradbury, and his reported need to store everything like a pack rat, her new house was filled with shelving that practically begged for Mia's collection. Jamming the sharp end of her scissors into the seam of a box labeled "Classics," Mia uncovered stories from her literature courses in college. Fingering the weathered spines of her favorites, she recalled her fascination when she was first introduced to Bradbury's short stories, such as "The Veldt" and "October

Country." She liked how the writing brought her into another world entirely—a world in which anything was possible, in which people could morph into creatures, heroes could be born out of everyday people, and the mysterious could be bravely explored.

Bradbury had a way of weaving his haunting stories with picturesque poetry. Mia had discovered a fondness for such fantastical creatures as Uncle Einar, and reread these magical stories often. In college, she got her hands on *Dandelion Wine* and *Fahrenheit 451*. Bradbury's prose had leapt off the page and pulled her into strange and frightening worlds, but she found the writing rich with significance and keen with observations on society. She admired the author for his passion as well as his foresight.

Just as Bradbury had been in his adult life, Mia was a regular fixture at the college library. She'd gobbled up everything from classics to contemporary novels. Her college years were about exploring, and the library had been her gateway. The writing came later, starting with bland reporting for the school newspaper, then slowly working her way into short stories with the help of an encouraging professor. She then dove into longer works of fiction. Sometimes her instructors would rave about her pages, sharing them with the class, but other times they criticized her work, making it a very confusing time to create. Ever since then, sharing her writing set Mia's self-confidence into an endless swinging pendulum, her heart rising and falling, depending upon the response her work received.

The day her novel, *Beautiful*, debuted, Mia was full of

nervous excitement. At thirty-five, it had taken her three years to complete, and many trying months searching for an agent and a book deal. *Beautiful* was a mixture of sweet and painful storytelling, depicting a man and his relationship with his philandering father. In hindsight, Mia sometimes wondered if her subconscious was channeling her own fears about her rocky relationship with Carson. She'd revealed uncomfortable bits and pieces of her private pain in that story without really comprehending it at the time. But she treasured the book, and her high-profile literary agent seemed to think it would do well. After less than stellar reviews and pitiful sales, the publisher dropped her, her agent went dark, and Mia was utterly defeated. She had wanted to crawl into a hole and stay there. Her darkest fears about being a writer had come true. She had exposed herself to the world and the world had ruthlessly chewed her up and spit her out. Maybe she wasn't supposed to be a novelist after all.

Following that, everything had spiraled downhill. She'd retreated to her bed, choosing to pull the shades down taut and pop sleeping pills while she hid in the shadows. She'd refused to return phone calls. Her depression became a deep chasm that she could not cross. Her sadness was too great, pushing out all those who tried to love her. She broke up with Carson, moved out of his cushy West Hollywood house, and retreated from her social life. The weight of her failures had been crushing.

Thankfully, Emma and Tom had taken her in with no questions asked. That was three years ago. Emma had doted on her sister with an almost obsessive passion. Mia was pretty sure Emma relished the whole thing. Emma had taken on the role as naturally as hopping back on an old familiar bike. And even though Mia was a grown woman, she was too passive to protest and thus gave control back to her directing sister.

A sharp knock at the door snapped Mia out of her unpacking haze. She startled back onto her heels and tipped the books into their box. As if her actions were connected to Mia's thoughts, Emma appeared in a cloud of impatience at the door.

"Hi," Emma said, breezing past her sister and into the front room. "Have you made any progress?" It sounded more like an accusation than a question. A pair of substantial tortoiseshell designer glasses swallowed up Emma's face, bouncing up and down as she talked. "I brought you some paint chips to consider for the exterior."

"Um, okay," Mia said. "Didn't know I needed paint chips, but thanks, I guess." Emma's Louis Vuitton tote was brimming over with what looked like fabric swatches and glossy catalogs. "Is there something else in that bag of yours for me, Mary Poppins?" she asked, trying to conceal a smirk.

"Well, as a matter of fact . . ." Emma pulled off her glasses and set the bag on the wood floor.

"Whoa!" Mia's hands flew to her mouth. "What's happening with your face?" Her sister's already tight visage was puffy and frozen at the same time, making her resemble something straight out of Madame Tussauds.

"Oh, please, Mia. It's not that dramatic." Emma replaced her glasses with a grumble. "Just a little Botox and some filler. It will settle down."

"Just a little Botox and some filler? Whatever you say." Mia knew her tone was cruel, but she couldn't help it. Her sister was starting to look like someone she didn't recognize. "Why do you need that stuff anyway? You're still young."

Emma snorted. "Young! I've got news for you honey—forty-two is not young in this town. Just wait until you're my age and then come talk to me." She thrust out a prideful chin and marched into the kitchen. Mia followed behind, wondering if it was the younger mothers at her kids'—Anna and Michael—school or Tom's perky-breasted students who made Emma feel old.

She was certainly a natural beauty, with her long honey-colored hair and model-worthy cheekbones. Emma was the eye-catching one of the family; everyone always said so. The constant reminder as a child had made Mia self-conscious about her plain features, her mousy brown coloring, and her hawkish profile. To compensate for this, Mia had been determined to shine in other ways: her studies and in her bookish creativity. But now that they were older, Mia knew her sister was sensitive about the deepening lines in her forehead and her rapidly changing figure. Emma was not one to wait around to grow old gracefully. If there was a needle that promised to deliver youth, she was going to plunk down serious cash to have it injected on a regular basis.

TWO HOURS LATER, AFTER HURRICANE EMMA HAD COME and gone, leaving heaps of decorator samples in her wake, Mia perched on her kitchen counter sipping tea. She knew her sister was right about updating things, but for now, Mia loved her ancient kitchen. She didn't want to erase the essence of Mr. Bradbury. She was sure that the author's spirit would speak to her as a writer somewhere in that house if she just stood still long enough to listen.

Nothing of the sort had happened yet. She'd spent the first week floating from room to room, sitting cross-legged on the floor, hoping to feel some kind of ghostly energy. After all, that's the reason she moved into the house—to glean new inspiration for her writing. But so far all she got was the sound of the house settling at night or the high-pitched squeaking the plumbing made whenever she ran the hot water.

Writing was always something that came naturally to Mia. Growing up, while neighborhood kids spent weekends playing kick the can in her palm tree–lined Southern California neighborhood, she preferred to sit in the shade and quietly make up new endings for fairy tales or design fake newspapers, which she would later hand out to her parents and anxiously wait for their review. It wasn't that she was a total introvert; she always had a cluster of playmates around and had fond memories of growing up on a street full of kids. But more often than not, she craved solitude, so she could read and create new stories. Emma, being four years older and forever the socialite, barely gave Mia the time of day back then, except to occasionally critique her outfit or to scoff at how messy Mia had let her bedroom become. While Emma was off planning school dances, Mia was home writing about the princess's ball. If her parents thought their two daughters' opposite choices of pastimes odd, they never said so.

Currently, Mia's dream of continuing her career as a novelist seemed to be stalling out. Like an engine that was out of fuel, she could not get her imagination to ignite. Her agent wasn't too interested in speaking with her again until she had something "fresh" to show him, and the idea of having to impress a new editor and publishing house felt daunting. She was in dire need of serious inspiration.

At the moment, a certain distraction in the form of her ex-fiancé was determined to get in the way. No matter how she'd tried to ignore Carson's pestering calls over the past days, she finally conceded and picked up her buzzing cell phone just before noon.

It wasn't so much of what Carson said as he exhaled with exasperation over finally reaching her, but rather the tone in which he said it that made her tense. "I want you to come in today," he said. "There's something we need to discuss."

"What is it?" Mia asked, nervously setting her tea on the counter. "I've just barely moved in and I'm knee-deep in boxes. It's not exactly a good time." She figured he'd call in a favor at some point, but this soon? A lump of dread materialized in her gut. "Seriously, Carson, what do you want?"

"I don't want to discuss it over the phone. You know how much I hate talking on the phone. Just come down before lunch. I'll have Karen order in that chicken salad you love. Good-bye." Click. He was gone, and had once again left her emotions in an all-too-familiar knot.

THREE

⌒

The office of Carson Cole was nothing if not intimidating. Located on the top floor of a gleaming Beverly Hills high-rise overlooking Wilshire Boulevard were the plush surroundings of one of Hollywood's most sought-after producers. The well-appointed suite, also known as the hub for Envision Entertainment, was a reflection of Carson's eclectic yet sophisticated taste. The four rooms that made up the suite, with their custom Italian sofas, hand-carved reclaimed wood coffee tables, and plasma TV screens on practically every wall, felt more like the interior of a luxury hotel than an office. Immaculately dressed assistants with Bluetooths scurried around like soldier ants making appointments and brewing espresso. Envision Entertainment videos boomed in full HD from every screen. And behind a set of beveled glass doors sat Carson, taking power meetings in his jeans and sneakers.

After making a name for himself with his action-packed blockbusters, *The Hero's Welcome* and *A Long Road Home*, he gained enough money and recognition to bring on a couple of director/partners, with whom he'd moved into the realm of rom-coms and family dramas. Carson was something of a jack-of-all-trades in the business, priding himself on discovering new talent and capitalizing on each actor's breakout role by launching them into stardom. The genre of film never really mattered to Carson. He genuinely loved movies and was fairly hands-on throughout each of his projects. His glaring flaw, however, was that he equally loved his female stars. And that shortcoming was something Mia was unwilling to overlook.

When she'd first met Carson five years ago, he was already a well-celebrated producer with high-grossing box-office hits. But the way he approached Mia, in the lobby of the Beverly Hills Hotel, was so genuine and charismatic that she couldn't help but be captivated. Of course she had known exactly who he was at the time; he was constantly in the media and a regular fixture on the red carpet events shown on TV. But one would never know it that September afternoon as this man, nearly ten years her senior, shifted from foot to foot in his untucked button-down and his baseball cap, asking Mia if he might sit down in the chair next to hers. Mia had tried to act casual and remain composed, even though her nerves were bouncing around like pogo sticks on the inside, as the famous moviemaker asked her name and inquired about her job. He'd said nothing of himself at the time, which Mia found refreshing. Unlike the rest of Beverly Hills, this man with the deep brown eyes and the day-old beard seemed to care more about the interests of others than he was in puffing himself up with importance. She was instantly attracted to his lean, muscular shoulders and strong jaw. Her subconscious may have worried that this handsome man was a player, but Mia was too woozy with lust to pay any attention.

She had been waiting around to interview a difficult decorator, on a freelance assignment by an expensive home magazine. The decorator turned out to be a no-show, and after an hour of conversation, Mia accepted Carson's invitation to dinner. Dinner led to drinks and long, sometimes blurred, conversation over wine into the wee hours. She had been completely transfixed with his easy smile and casual charm.

Three years and an engagement ring later, after she'd moved into his über-private estate, tucked away in the chic Bird Streets neighborhood of West Hollywood, Mia found herself suddenly alone. She was living in a big house surrounded by luxury, but more often than not there was no one to share it with. She felt isolated, like a princess locked away in a beautiful but unfriendly tower. Carson worked strange hours, entertained too much, and to her devastation, admitted to multiple affairs with leading ladies. But as awful as things had become, Mia still missed him from time to time. There had been such romance in the beginning and no one ever seemed to champion Mia as much as Carson had. For all of his faults, he was quite supportive of Mia and used to remind her on a daily basis that she had talent. According to all of his friends, he'd never gotten over losing her. For these reasons alone, Mia and Carson had managed to remain friends after the breakup.

Now, walking through the glass doors into Carson's office, Mia felt like the principal was summoning her. He always had a way of being just needy enough with an edge of authority to get Mia to come when he came calling. "He needs me," she had once tried to explain to Emma after Carson had called with late-night anxiety about a film that was about to premiere.

"Just like he needs to put his manhood into every wannabe actress that crosses his path?" Emma could cut right into Mia's wound every time. That particular argument had led to a weeklong stalemate with her sister until the two of them agreed to not discuss Carson in the future. Emma had stated she'd rather not know what her sister's ex was up to if she could help it. Tom had only shrugged and offered an apologetic smile from behind the breakfast counter. Emma's house. Emma's rules.

So, with a sense of duty as familiar as an old coat, Mia showered and changed and appeared in Carson's world right on time.

"Jesus, you look gorgeous," he said, springing up from behind his mammoth desk to embrace her.

"Give it a rest, Carson," she said, flopping down in an armchair. She'd managed to slip on a flattering sundress and apply just a touch of lip gloss before she'd dashed out of the house, but she wasn't about to acknowledge that she'd made an effort. "I'm here. What is it that couldn't possibly wait?"

"First, how's the house? Everything you wanted?" He rested on the corner of his polished desk and leaned forward. There was an edge to his voice.

"Yes, it's great. Thanks." She didn't like his vaguely masked attempt at reminding her he'd done her a favor. She felt uneasy, expecting she was in for some bad news. Balling up her fists into her lap, she tried to hide her growing anxiety.

"Great. So glad it worked out," he said.

"Carson, I've told you a thousand times I'm grateful for the loan," she said. "You're welcome to come see the place anytime." She was rambling now, trying to head off whatever was coming.

"Yeah, I know. That's not what this is about." He ran his palm through a thick tuft of dusty brown hair. Mia missed that hair. The earthy way it smelled with a twinge of something that reminded her of cedar. Realizing she was fixating on his hair, she snapped back into focus and squinted, trying to concentrate on what he was saying. "I need your help with a sensitive project. With something kind of . . . uh . . . classified for lack of a better term."

"Classified? Like a secret agent? Is this for a movie?" Maybe he was offering her a screenwriting job. They had talked about never working together when they were a couple, but now that they were separated, perhaps things had changed.

"Yes . . . well, no. Not exactly." He was beginning to stutter. Now it was Carson who looked uneasy. He took a panicky breath. "I need help with an actress."

Mia was on her feet before Carson could blink. Memories shot like rapid-fire bullets into her brain: photos of Carson kissing another woman, screaming matches in their living room, packed suitcases. She was stumbling backward, toward the door. "No way, Carson! You're delusional if you think I'm going to counsel you through one of your messy bimbo breakups!" She was only vaguely aware that she was shouting now, the blood pumping loudly in her ears. "I said I'd return a favor, but not this!" She turned on her heel to storm out but Carson grabbed her shoulder.

"Whoa! Hold on," he said. "Geez, Mia, I think you're jumping to conclusions."

She turned to face him, ready to bolt. "Well, you better explain quickly, because I'm about to leave."

He shoved his hands in his pockets and glanced at the ground like a guilty schoolboy. "I'm sorry for everything, and you know that. I didn't mean to upset you, I swear." He was pacing now. "But you're always the one I can count on, and right now I need a little help." Mia folded her arms tight and braced for what he was about to tell her.

"Look, the production company has gotten into a bit of a pickle. We're scheduled to start filming *Beyond Daybreak* in a month and our contracted actress, our star actress, has just exited rehab."

Typical, Mia thought. "Keep going," she said, unwilling to budge.

"Well, long story short is we paid a lot of money to insure her and now, well, the director is having some doubts and we sort of need, well, a . . ."

"A what, Carson? Spit it out." She was beyond annoyed.

"We need a mentor." He shrank back into a loveseat and threw his hands into the air. "We need a babysitter, all right?

We need someone who can guide this young girl and keep her out of trouble and basically keep an eye on her."

Mia took a step closer and peered into her ex's nervous expression. "I'm sorry, it's been a long week," she said. "Did you just say you need me to babysit an addict for you?" Well, this was a first. Of all the scenarios that Mia could have concocted in her head, taking care of an unstable actress was definitely not one of them. She wasn't sure if she should be outraged or amused.

"Ugh, don't start talking to me like you're Emma." He rolled his eyes. "Just sit down and let me explain. I promise, it's not what you think." He paused and gestured toward a chair. "Please, Mia."

"Fine," she said, flopping down again. "But you better have my chicken salad."

FOUR

⌒

et me get this straight," Mia said through a mouthful of lettuce. "You want me to take in *the* Zoe Winter, as in the DUI-getting, club-hopping actress who's on the cover of the tabloids every other week?" This was unbelievable. One minute she was unpacking her belongings in her quiet little house on a hill and the next being asked to rent out a room to one of Hollywood's most notorious starlets. It couldn't possibly end well. She'd recently read about the sloppy antics of another drunken Hollywood celebrity, and this girl's situation didn't seem all that different.

"Yes, that is exactly what I'm asking," Carson said. He hunched over and took a wolf-sized bite of his veggie burger, as though it was any other regular lunch meeting. Did he make these kinds of deals all the time? Since when did the line blur between making sure movies made it to making sure actresses made it? She didn't want to know. Probably a trend that started with Marilyn Monroe and has been an industry norm ever since.

Carson continued, "I'm not asking you to hold her hand every minute of the day. But this girl hasn't got any reliable family and she's just newly clean. She needs a leg up." Clean. What did that even mean? Like she'd been run through the dishwasher and was ready for use now? And how did Carson even know if this girl was truly intoxicant-free anyway?

"So, what was she on? Pills or something?" Mia had read articles stating how the twentysomethings were known as the Ritalin Generation, sharing prescription pills with one another as though they were boxes of Tic Tacs. It was only a matter of time before they moved on to heavier narcotics, many unable to kick the habit.

Carson must have been reading her worried expression. "She's had problems with alcohol, mostly, but there were some pill issues too." Issues? Mia was going to have to go home and google "Zoe Winter pill issues" and see what popped up. She made a mental note to get the cable guy up to the house sooner rather than later.

"So, what if she's not really sober? What then? Am I going to have some kind of incident in my house? What if she's violent?" Did her bedroom even have a lock on the door? Not able to remember, she made another note to call a locksmith.

He moved a massive burger wad to one side of his mouth. "Okay. First, she's a very sweet kid. Second, I believe she's sober and wants to stay that way. Just meet her and you can judge for yourself." He downed the remainder of his meal with a swig of his Arnold Palmer. He devoured food without hesitation, the same way he devoured women. Watching him, Mia felt that old familiar angst creep up her spine.

"I don't get it. Why me? Don't you have some kind of handler for a job like this?"

"No, I don't have handlers. I'm not the Mob, Mia." He set his lunch aside and brushed crumbs from his pants. "This is a good kid who caught a couple of bad breaks. She's got a huge following and the studio needs this movie to be a blockbuster. We've got a lot riding on this project and I need to see it through. You know I don't trust too many people. I'm asking you to do me this favor. It's not forever. Just a few months." He hesitated, considering her. "And who knows, maybe she'll want you to ghostwrite her memoir or something." He let the last bit hang in the air like a dangling carrot.

Mia didn't bite. "Her memoir? Get serious. What is she, like, twenty-two? What could she possibly have to say that would fill a book?" Mia palmed her forehead, annoyed at the notion that any clueless celebrity could publish a book when it took dedicated writers like her years to get noticed.

"She's twenty-three and she might have a lot to say. I bet that agent of yours would jump at the chance to rep her book." Carson pointed a finger like Mia should be taking notes.

Mia wondered what exactly this girl had on Carson to make him this committed to her well-being. Was it really all about studio contracts and the big money attached to the project? Sure, she wished Carson success and knew how crucial it was for him to be tied to a box-office hit. But just how much did this young actress mean to him? The thought of witnessing another salacious Hollywood affair starring her ex-fiancé gave Mia the sweats. Raising a moist palm, Mia fought the urge to fan herself. Squaring her shoulders, she regained a bit of composure. "Yeah, well, I'll think about it," she said.

"Don't think about it. Just say yes," Carson said. "Look, I know you want to do some renovations to the house. I'll make sure the studio pays a hefty amount to rent a room to Zoe. You'll be making money and making me happy by doing this. Please say you'll do it." There he was again with that easy smile.

"Okay, she can stay," she said, eyeing him. "But after this, we're even."

FORTY-FIVE MINUTES LATER, AFTER WINDING HER WAY through the unfriendly congestion of Los Angeles traffic, a weary Mia arrived home. As she emerged from her car, a glint of white near the front door caught her eye. Curious as to its contents, she climbed the stone steps and came to a halt at an unassuming business-sized envelope fastened just above the doorbell. It was mysteriously blank on the outside, neatly taped shut and folded with care. Running her finger along the seam, she split open the envelope to reveal a small square of paper, a scrap really, and on it a small winged dragon with jagged talons and a razor-thin body stared back at her. Turning the paper over, she studied it. No note, no signature, just a pencil sketch. Odd. Who could have left this?

Glancing over her shoulder, Mia surveyed the tree-lined

street. All was still. Not a car or neighbor in sight. She tried to picture Bradbury on this very street, peddling his bike with his shock of white hair blowing about, on his way to visit the library. She wondered if he liked to stop and talk with passersby or if he ever quoted poetry aloud as he went. On the other side the door a faint ringing broke her daydream. She fumbled with her key and raced inside.

Locating her cell phone on the stairs, she answered. "Hello?"

"It's about time!" An irritated Emma greeted her on the other end. "Don't you ever answer your phone?"

Mia kicked off her sandals and leaned against the wall. "Hey," she said. "Sorry, I guess I forgot to bring my phone with me."

"Mia," Emma scolded. "Why can't you be like a normal person and carry your cell phone with you when you leave the house?"

"Sorry, I forgot," she said. "I was in a hurry this morning, that's all."

"Hurry for where?" Emma never was able to ask Mia a question without it sounding like it was an interrogation.

"Oh, just running errands," Mia fumbled. She was not ready to reveal to her overprotective sister that her ex-fiancé just asked her to house a newly reformed drug addict. Somehow, Mia did not envision that conversation going well.

"You're acting strange," Emma said. "Are you feeling all right?"

Mia sighed. "Yes. Just got a lot to do right now, that's all."

Like move all of her clutter and make up the futon for her soon-to-be tenant. Where were her extra sheets, anyway? Was she required to provide towels? Just how did one prepare for the arrival of a newly released rehab patient? She needed to get rid of Emma and find out.

FIVE

⌐

*L*ying in bed that night, under a borrowed quilt from Emma's house, Mia fingered the mysterious dragon drawing that had been taped to her door and pondered its significance. It had hauntingly familiar elements, with its defined talons and batlike wings, reminiscent of the creatures from Bradbury's stories. But she couldn't figure out what the image meant. She'd assumed that it had something to do with the author. He had lived in the house for several decades and the address was no secret to the general public. Perhaps it was just left by a fan or tourist who maybe didn't realize the house now belonged to someone new. Perhaps it was someone's way of paying homage to the artist, the way people left bottles of booze at Jim Morrison's grave. If this were the case, she felt like she should keep it. But where? Placing it on her bedside table, she decided to think about it more in the morning.

What followed was a restless night. Paper dragons, cloaked in darkness, crept into Mia's dreams. They charged about with billowy smoke seeping from their nostrils, their talons scraping the dry earth beneath them. Each new image came in and out of focus, like an old-fashioned movie reel. From where they were coming or going Mia couldn't decipher. It was only when a shuttered window started banging from somewhere in the house that she was jolted awake, pajamas soaked with sweat as she groped blindly for the lamp.

Clap! Clap! The shutters banged to the rhythm of the wind. Switching on the light, Mia blinked the sleepy fog from her thoughts and tried to get her bearings. The vicious Santa Ana winds, that seemed to come out of nowhere, were blowing across the Southern California landscape that autumn. The forceful blasts had caused the temperature to rise and make it necessary to open the windows. She must have forgotten to secure the kitchen shutters before bed and a gust had probably forced something loose. She rubbed her half-shut eyes and padded across the uneven floorboards and into the shadowy hallway.

Mia quickened her pace, now fully aware of her surroundings. Following the noise, she discovered a pair of weathered shutters flung open in the dining room. Not remembering opening this particular window, she shivered against the now cooling temperature and secured it shut. A faint howling, like a distant melancholy mourning, whistled through the old iron grate in the wall. *Banshee*, Mia instantly thought. Were these eerie callings in the night wind those of Bradbury's "Banshee" in his short story of Irish adventure? That of the female spirit who called out to lonely souls in the dead of night? Mia's bare toes grew icy against the hard floor, and she was keenly aware of her arm hair standing on end. It wasn't that she was so much afraid, but more that she sensed a haunting presence, an unsettling reminder of something yet to come.

"Out you go!" she shouted at no one in particular. Mia whacked her hands together for good measure. Only a hollow echo answered back. *Tea,* she told herself. *You need to wake up with some hot tea.*

With just a trace of moonlight peeking through the wooden slats to guide her, she made her way through the dining room doors and across a small, blue-tiled room to the kitchen. She was comforted with how the floors felt against her bare feet. The square tiles with their vintage flower design were one of her favorite parts of the house. Some of the porcelain was worn down in spots, perhaps revealing a pattern of the Bradbury family routine over the last fifty years. It pleased Mia to feel these surfaces, as though she was following in a loved one's footsteps, assured by their existence.

Not wanting to turn on the lights, she decided on a designer candle Emma had left near the sink. The match hissed alive with its orange glow. For once, she was grateful for her sister's insistence on leaving a few luxuries around the house during her last visit. The scent of gardenias floated through the room. Mia's favorite. Gratitude sparked in her heart. Sometimes Emma really did have her best interest in mind.

Reaching for the upper cabinets, she fished out a box of tea. Again, the rough, worn surface of the cabinet knobs pleased her. An overhaul of the fixtures would come in time but for now these small things made her feel less lonely. Lighting the fire under her stainless steel kettle, she leaned back against the counter and wondered more about the dragon drawing. Did Bradbury draw much? She couldn't remember. Someone else always illustrated his books. But winged creatures were part of his world for sure. Suddenly inspired, Mia jumped to find her journal in the living room. She needed to write down her thoughts on the matter before daybreak came and motivation faded.

THE WHIR OF A LAWNMOWER AWAKENED MIA THE next day. The first thing she noticed was her stiff neck, having fallen asleep on the unforgiving arm of the room's lone loveseat. Mia rubbed her puffy eyes and gingerly stretched her limbs. The lamp above her head glowed, its bulb a meager second to the bright daylight that now streamed into the front room. Confused, she glanced around for a clock. How long had she been asleep? She noticed her half-full journal lying askew on the floor, the uncapped pen nearby. Wandering into the kitchen, she discovered the candle still barely going, long drips of congealed wax spilled over the glass base. Her phone lay on the counter. Pressing the power button, she read 8:20 a.m.

Still bleary and wanting to make a fresh cup of tea, Mia was only half alert when a sharp knocking came at the front door. Who on earth could that be this early? Emma, no doubt. Muttering, she shuffled into the foyer and leaned hard on the door as she worked the old lock.

"Carson!" Mia jumped back. "What are you doing here?" She was suddenly sensitive of her morning breath and uncombed hair. Carson never stopped by unannounced. It wasn't his style. He'd always preferred people to plan for his arrival. Had she forgotten they had an appointment? Her brain tried to shift gears from the thought that she wasn't fully dressed to her day's calendar.

On the opposite end of the spectrum, a starched and hypercaffeinated Carson breezed past his ex-girlfriend and toured the house without invitation. His polished Cole Haans made a loud tapping noise as he moved from one room to another in haste.

"So this is the famous Ray Bradbury house," he said more to himself than anyone else. "Good god, Mia. You've got your work cut out for you." He glimpsed at one of the many bookshelves. He paused in the front room and raised an eyebrow. "This is what cost me a million and a half bucks?"

Mia shut the door and slumped onto what was now becoming her regular seat on the stairs. She considered answering him, but he continued into overdrive and marched through the dining area and breakfast room and on into the dated kitchen, mumbling something she couldn't quite hear. She leaned back and let him have the run of the house, like an anxious terrier in search of a lost ball.

After he covered the first level, he charged past her to the upstairs rooms. After a minute he called down. "Which one is for Zoe?"

Oh damn! That's why he's here, Mia thought. *He's scouting out a location for his prized actress.* Mia had hardly thought about the girl's accommodations, let alone done anything about them.

"Um, that one in the middle, I guess." She cringed as she said it, knowing he'd soon discover the heap of half-open boxes and the dusty old rug blocking the door. A few more steps sounded, then they paused.

"Holy shit! Look at these bathrooms! This is straight out of the 1950s, Mia!" he called down like it was supposed to be news to her.

"Charm!" she shouted back. "That's the whole point, you snob."

Carson returned, looking dumbfounded. "Where's your room?" His head swiveled around like an owl on the hunt.

"I've taken the Bradburys' old room." She pointed her finger toward the far end of the house. "It's got doors leading to a nice patio." When she first moved in, she wasn't sure which room to take. It felt odd to sleep in the room Bradbury and his wife had slept in. Did she dare take over such a sacred space? She'd considered setting up camp in what the real estate flyer designated as the maid's quarters, but that room seemed too tight. The Bradburys' room was on the main level and let in the most natural light. It had warm wood floors, plenty of shelf space, and a funny old mirrored vanity in the bathroom. In addition to this, a good-sized grass area stretched beyond the brick patio, giving Mia hope that she could exercise her green thumb come spring.

For the first time since he'd walked in the door, Carson asked permission before he went in search of her bedroom. She waved him off like a patient schoolteacher and waited for his return.

"Still don't like to make your bed, huh?" he asked a few minutes later. She noticed he had lingered in that room the longest.

"Um . . . well . . . I got up in the middle of the night to some weird noises and slept in the living room instead." She stood now and gestured to the love seat.

"What kind of noises?" He suddenly looked alarmed. "Are you safe here? Was someone outside?" He moved to the front door again and jiggled it.

"Don't get all frantic," she said. "Just the Santa Anas, that's all."

He didn't look convinced, but he stopped fiddling with the lock long enough to explain his reason for coming. "Zoe's getting out in two days, Mia. I've told her that my good friend, the novelist, will be taking her in for a bit. She seems open to the idea." His eyebrows hovered as he waited for an equally optimistic response.

Mia frowned. "Well, goody for her. What about me? I'm supposed to get her room ready in two days?" She was incredulous. How would she have time to clear her storage out, acquire bedding and towels, and arrange for a house cleaner in two short days?

As he headed for the door, Carson brushed her cheek with a hurried kiss. "It's happening, Mia. I suggest you get the lead out."

SIX

⌣

$\mathcal{E}$mma couldn't have been more thrilled when Mia had inquired about the use of her house cleaner. Rocio had been with the Hutter family for seven years and was a staple in their household. It was with pure glee that Emma arrived on Mia's doorstep, with mops, sprays, and a husky Rocio at her side. In true Emma fashion, she was horrified at the news of Mia's arrangement with Carson, but was willing to "fluff up" the guest room before the new tenant moved in.

"I had to rearrange my whole morning, but I'm here!" The cheer in her voice led Mia to believe that this might be the best part of her overenthusiastic sister's day.

"Thanks," she said. "Hi, Rocio. Welcome to my new home." She stepped aside as the two unloaded their cleaning gear and what looked like bags of linens into the foyer.

"Nice house, Miss Mia." Rocio nodded. She was a woman of few words, something Mia could appreciate.

"Well, no time to dillydally," Emma broke in. "Let's get to work."

For the remainder of the day, Mia did what she did best when her sister was in decorator mode: she got out of her way. With two very overdue freelance stories due for a women's magazine, and a rising panic about her lack of productivity, she swiftly excused herself and made her way to the refuge of the den to write at her computer.

The home had two living rooms, in Mia's opinion. The lower room had lovely vaulted ceilings, bookshelves, high windows, and a stately yet inviting brick fireplace. It was the perfect place to entertain guests. But the den was special for other reasons. It was there in the lesser-sized living room, with its aged built-ins, wainscoted walls, and humble corner fireplace, that Bradbury was often photographed surrounded by piles of papers, books, and artifacts that he'd collected throughout his career. Before she'd moved in, Mia had googled videos of the author being interviewed in this very room. She'd watched these clips over and over again, often taking notes on the precious advice he doled out to the camera.

Although it was documented that Bradbury did the majority of his work in the cavernous unfinished basement one level below, Emma had no inclination to follow suit. A creaky, narrow staircase dropped down into a large series of chambers in a dank setting. The basement was void of natural light, because the only window and door were boarded over to make room for more shelving. Each section was divided by bookshelf after bookshelf. Mia knew the author valued this portion of the house, and because of this he probably oozed out much of his genius in that basement.

But to Mia, it was a touch too dark and creepy, a dungeon of sorts. Plus, she wasn't sure she had it in her to give the basement the TLC it so badly needed.

Instead, when she'd moved in, there was no doubt in her mind that her small reclaimed wood desk (a gift she'd bought herself with the advance from her novel) would live in the den, along with her computer and her books on the craft of writing. The only other accouterments she had added to the cozy room were a spice-colored area rug and a brushed nickel floor lamp on loan from Emma's house. She wanted to feel like the room was already full with Bradbury's spirit. It didn't need to be overrun with her things, at least not quite yet.

As she pounded out on her keyboard the benefits and treatments available at a popular women's spa—which was ironic given the fact Mia hadn't pampered herself in years—she was only vaguely aware of the shuffling and banging just outside the door. From what she imagined, Rocio and Emma were putting some serious elbow grease into Zoe's portion of the house. Leaning in, she selected the "chill out" music station pretuned to her computer and upped her speaker's volume in an effort to drown out the world outside.

Writing was a solitary sport, and that's exactly the way Mia liked it. She knew fellow writers who preferred to sit in crowded coffee shops to work, and others who liked to light a joint or a stick of incense to get the inspiration going. For Mia, the best recipe was a little bit of chocolate (she faithfully kept a stash of neatly wrapped miniatures in her desk drawer) and complete and total isolation. Once, when they were living together, Carson made the mistake of resting his haunches on the edge of her desk, absentmindedly flipping through her pencil jar as he told her about his day. It took Mia all of thirty seconds to inform him that he was harshing her mellow. Fraternizing with this writer was not allowed during work hours. Carson had protested that she didn't have any set work hours per se and that it was impossible to know when he was allowed to approach her. Her reply was that if she was at her desk, then she was at work.

Looking back, Mia wondered if excluding Carson from her creative life alienated him more than he had let on. More than once, he gave a stung look when she'd banished him from her desk. Maybe she had been too rigid with him. But hadn't he been the one to run around town with a secret "work life" of his own? She shook her head and tried to focus back on the details of her article.

Just when she was going over a bit of research, she heard a soft knock on the door. "Mia, we're done," Emma said from the other side. "You want to come see?"

Annoyed at the interruption, Mia conceded and appeared halfheartedly in the hallway. Right away, a waxy pine scent greeted her. On one side of the bedroom door stood a flushed-face Rocio, and on the other side stood Emma, who was grinning like the Cheshire cat.

"Well, let's see what this Zoe girl is going to get," Mia announced as she entered. What she discovered took her breath away. The once desolate room was now like a page out of a home furnishings catalog. A mod-style upholstered bed, with muted gray bedding in downy layers and oversized chenille pillows, rested in the center of the room. At the end were a little tufted bench and a thick, cozy wool throw. The worn wood floors were newly polished and the windows were thrown wide open to allow for the mild breeze. Next to the bed stood a precious mirrored nightstand holding a delicate vase of blushing tulips. The whole look was retro and modern and feminine—exactly what Mia would imagine a twenty-three-year-old starlet would love.

Spinning around, she regarded Emma with wide eyes. "It's perfect!" she said. "You totally transformed the place, but still respected the character of the house! Where did all this furniture come from?" Mia only just realized the absence of her tired futon.

"Didn't you hear the moving guys coming down the stairs?" Emma asked.

"I guess my music was louder than I realized," Mia said. "But I can't afford this stuff." Anxiety crept in, hot and prickly under her skin.

"Don't you worry about it," Emma said. "My friend Jeannie . . . You remember Jeannie from the club don't you? Anyway, she stages homes and she owed me a favor. She said she's happy to loan you the furniture as long as you let her come take photographs of her work in the house of Ray Bradbury." Emma beamed like she'd just come up with a cure for a fatal disease.

"Um . . . okay . . . I guess." Mia's shoulders collapsed a bit. She wasn't sure how she felt about some stranger wheedling her way into a former celebrity's house to snap photos. The house was too special to be exploited in such a way. But the work was already done, so how much could she really protest?

Emma had made the deal and there was no denying her. Mia had zero interest in knowing what kind of "favors" these country club wives held over one another. With a sigh, she nodded in agreement.

As bags and buckets were lugged through the front entrance, Emma stopped short to study something. "It seems that someone's left you a funny little drawing," she said, yanking at a small piece of white paper taped to the doorbell. She looked at it and wrinkled her nose as if she'd been forced to look at something obscene.

Stepping out to investigate, Mia saw that it was a pencil drawing. On it, a spindly branched tree blew in the wind, its reedy limbs heavy with jack-o'-lanterns. There was no color, no shading even, just a simple figure on a bare page. She studied the sketch for a moment, searching her brain for a faraway recollection. After a pause, she tapped the paper with her finger. "Halloween Tree," she said. She handled the paper and looked out past Emma. The street remained still, not a soul in sight.

"What the heck is a Halloween tree?" Emma asked, her face still scrunched.

"You know, Ray Bradbury's story about the boys who go out on Halloween only to have their friend whisked away?" Noting Emma's confusion, Mia pocketed the sketch until later. "Well, at least that's what it reminds me of."

Emma shrugged. "Can't say that I know that one. Why is it at your door? Are people bothering you?" she asked, the mother in her voice coming out.

"I'm not sure," Mia replied.

SEVEN

⌒

The arrival of Zoe Winter held less fanfare than Mia had expected. At nine o'clock the next morning, a black SUV with darkened windows and shiny chrome wheels pulled up to the curb and waited with the motor idling. Awakened by the whipping winds several hours earlier, Mia rose, feeling unsettled as she tugged a fleece sweatshirt over her tangled nest of hair and set about pacing the living room. For the next few hours she wrung her hands in anticipation, a laundry list of particulars running like ticker tape through her head. Had the guest bath enough soap? Would the timeworn closet be sufficient to hold the wardrobe of an actress? Should she light a few gardenia candles to chase out the smell of old house?

As she fussed over pillows and refolded kitchen towels, the clock on her mantle ticked like a waiting time bomb. She was aware of the restless trees outside, swaying and tilting with the wind, their frantic waving serving as a warning. At the last minute, Mia decided to cautiously close the door to the den. Her office was to be off-limits. It was her place of work and strangers were not welcome there. More than that, Mia felt it was her duty to protect that portion of the house. It had been one of Bradbury's favorite spots, where he housed his beloved artifacts and kept his mementos. If the old man's spirit existed anywhere, it was in that room. No dim-witted starlet was going to traipse around such a sacred space, Mia told herself. Not on her watch.

She hovered at the dining room window and watched the still-running car. Nothing happened for several minutes, and Mia wondered if the girl inside was having second thoughts. Who goes to live with a total stranger anyway? Maybe this Zoe person was ready to flee, rapidly punching out the phone numbers of all her friends, begging for assistance. Perhaps she felt like staying at this old-fashioned, quirky yellow house that belonged to some spinster writer was some kind of punishment or ridiculous test to remain sober, doled out by the production company. It wasn't as if Mia hadn't wondered the same thing.

Finally, a glimmering silver Mercedes rounded the corner and eased behind the parked car. "Carson, thank god," Mia said aloud. Her fingers loosened their grip on the sill at the sight of him. Even though it was a Saturday, Carson appeared annoyingly polished in his dark-washed jeans and crewneck sweater. The wind traveled down the street in sweeping gusts, causing his well-groomed hair to blow back a bit, giving him a boyish look. Mia could almost smell the cedar aftershave from where she stood. Her heart quickened a beat. Swallowing hard, she reminded herself to remain calm.

Approaching the back of the SUV, Carson rapped on the door with his knuckles. The tinted glass window rolled down halfway, revealing a head of amber-colored hair. Carson said something to the person inside, turned, and gestured to the house. "Shit!" Mia ducked down, hoping he hadn't noticed her spying. She hugged her knees and counted to five before she ventured a second peek through the wooden shades.

By the time she righted herself, Mia discovered a small pack of people traveling up her front steps. Her eyes darted from face to face, trying to decipher who was approaching. Leading the troupe was Carson, taking quick but uneasy steps. Following him was a tall brunette woman who appeared to be in her forties. She spoke into a cell phone and had a mound of dry cleaning bags draped over her arm. The woman marched along in a pencil skirt and stilettos like a soldier in designer clothing. On her left was the head of auburn hair, attached to a petite frame wearing a checkered black shirt and black jeans with matching combat boots. Mia couldn't make out her face, as it was bowed down, almost hiding from the sunlight. Pulling up the rear was a hulking bouncer type in a bad leather jacket and an equally unfortunate expression. Mia guessed this was the bodyguard. As the doorbell chimed, she moved at what felt like the speed of molasses to answer.

The next ten minutes were a blur. Carson practically let himself in, escorting the entourage through the house, speaking in a loud tour guide manner. The woman on the phone introduced herself as Zoe's agent, Sharon. She shook Mia's hand firmly and thrust the stack of dry cleaning bags in her direction, saying something about retrieving more from the car. The bodyguard remained silent, scouring the place with suspicious eyes, then stepping aside to guide his client farther into the house. It wasn't until the front door clicked shut that brief introductions were made. The small girl in the middle finally met Mia's gaze and offered a meek smile.

She was stunning. Even with her pale cheeks and dreary clothes, Zoe Winter had dark green eyes that sparkled like no jewel Mia had ever seen. Her long, wavy hair was parted in the middle, framing round cheeks with the hint of a dimple on either side. Her pouty lips pushed back to expose one crooked tooth that, to Mia, made her even more interesting. She reminded Mia of a wounded forest animal, lovely to look at but weary and skittish from a life on the run. Having zero motherly instincts, Mia didn't know whether to hug the girl or shoo her to her room. Instead, she continued to stare and say nothing.

"Ahem!" Carson broke the silence, shifting uncomfortably in the hallway. "So, Zoe here would probably like to get settled. Why don't you be the one to show her to her room?" He raised his eyebrows and waited for Mia to react.

"Oh! Right," she said, lurching forward. "It's this way." Mia moved down the corridor and checked over her shoulder to see if the scared animal was following. Zoe shuffled behind, her chipped onyx nails clutching a bejeweled cell phone.

"Wait for me!" Sharon ran click-clacking up the stairs in her impossibly high heels, a designer duffle bag under each arm. This woman was clearly winded and not used to carting around someone else's luggage. But Mia guessed that this was likely the one prized client for whom Sharon was willing to hustle.

The floorboards groaned under the arrival of the three women. Stepping aside to let Zoe view the bedroom, Mia held her breath and watched for a response. It was silly to wish for a complete stranger's approval. This girl was likely used to swanky accommodations more like the Chateau Marmont, not a 1930s relic in the middle of the suburbs. But after a minute of painful silence, the girl nodded and smiled. Relieved, Mia excused herself and scurried back down to find Carson for her next set of instructions.

AFTER THREE DAYS AND MULTIPLE EPISODES OF pressing her ear to the door of her new houseguest, Mia's jumpy fingers punched Carson's number on speed dial on her phone. At first she had been leery of Zoe, who locked herself in the guest room with little to say other than a brief "Thank you" when Mia wished her a good night's sleep. Mia had expected some of the girl's behavior, like the wailings of melancholy music vibrating through the walls, the light spilling from her room at all hours of the night, and the tomblike silence during the day, suggesting that like any other young person, Zoe was fond of sleeping through the morning.

Mia barely knew the girl existed, save for the small evidence of yogurt containers in the kitchen trash and cracker crumbs on the counter. It was like living in the company of a skittish nocturnal creature, rarely exposed in daylight, little traces left behind from midnight scavenging. Mia went from uncertain to worried in the span of a few days. Carson should be notified of what a mistake this whole experiment really was.

He answered in half a ring. "What's up?"

"We need to talk."

"I've got an interview starting, so you have thirty seconds." She was getting the work voice. Mia detested being on the receiving end of this terse manner. There was a small sliver of Carson that acted like Johnny Hollywood during the day, a real wheeler and dealer making things happen. Nothing turned her off more.

She sighed deeply in the receiver. "Fine. The short version is that your protégée is acting creepy and I'm not sure that it's working out." Silence. She couldn't tell if he was contemplating or distracted. "Carson?"

There was some rustling on the other end, followed by a muffled voice. "Yes, I'm here."

"Are you with someone?" A familiar angst began gnawing at her insides. Catching Carson in the middle of one of his female encounters was always something that she was afraid of doing. "I can call you back."

"Yes, I told you I'm getting ready for an interview. It's for the entertainment news channel. The makeup gal is powdering my forehead."

"How very masculine." She smiled, the gnawing subsiding a little.

"Mia, get serious. What's wrong with Zoe? What do you mean she's creeping you out?"

"She hasn't come out of her room for days, and god knows what she's doing in there all night. Did anyone even check her bag for substances before she got here?" Her voice pitched higher with each word, making her sound too much like a yipping Chihuahua.

This time it was Carson who sighed. "First of all, calm down. Second of all, it's only been three days. The girl just got out of rehab. She's probably exhausted. And not that it's any of your business, but yes, the facility checks the bags of all their residents."

She hated being told to calm down, but she knew her ex well enough not to pick a fight over the phone. Instead she tried to appeal with her intuition. "I don't know, Carson. I have a funny feeling."

"Have you even tried to talk to her? Why don't you knock on her door and offer her some of that damn tea you're always drinking? Make friends." He was patronizing her, clearly not pleased with the interruption.

"You're making me sound like a nervous Nellie."

"You *are* a nervous Nellie. Look, I gotta go. Just try and relax and I'll call you later." The connection went dead. He was gone. Mia flopped back onto the bed and listened to the deafening silence.

EIGHT

⌐

*O*n the fourth night of Zoe's arrival, the two women had a genuine encounter. Mia considered it an encounter because of the quality of the short visit they shared in the kitchen just before midnight. She'd been standing at the sink, gazing out into the inky blackness of the night with her hands wrapped around a steaming mug of tea. Unable to shut her eyes because the Santa Anas had picked up again, sending moans and creaks up through the air vents, Mia had tossed her sheets into a jumble before giving up on the idea of sleep. Reaching for her sheer cotton robe, she made a swift tie around her waist and felt her way down the darkened hallway.

The kitchen had become one of her favorite places of solace on nights like these. The unfamiliar ways in which the house settled at night still put her on edge, like waiting for the arrival of an unwelcome guest. Trying to sleep through the noises only sent her to wade through fitful dreams of imaginary dragons and winged creatures flapping about. It was during these moments that she would wake with a start, worrying about the unreachable girl one floor above or the odd drawings left at her door. She couldn't work out the meaning of either, and it disturbed her more than she liked.

On the night that their paths collided, Mia had felt a fleeting presence in the room. Like a whisper that traveled delicately across a breeze, Zoe had padded with light feet into the kitchen and waited to be noticed. At this development, a blip of hope brightened inside Mia. Turning around with care so as not to frighten off her visitor, Mia smiled and offered a friendly nod.

"Hi there," she said. "Feel like a cup of tea?"

The girl balanced on the balls of her feet as if she might turn and run, her onyx toenails mirroring the same moody polish as her chipped fingers. She scanned from Mia's cup to the counter behind her. "Um, I'm not much of a tea drinker, but sure. I guess." This girl wore her indecision like an uncomfortable jacket.

Mia very much wanted to meet Zoe's eyes. She needed to judge what kind of person she was dealing with. She had secretly looked up some signs of drug abuse online earlier in the day, on the off chance that she'd have to put her case before Carson again. To her relief, Zoe met her glance with a sober expression and she stepped farther into the kitchen, propping herself on the counter next to Mia.

"My mom drinks tea," Zoe said. "But I'm more of a coffee person."

The sudden offer of personal information felt like an opening to Mia. "Oh, what kind of tea does your mom like?"

Mia moved quickly, filling the kettle and lighting the stove.

"I don't really know. I think something with the word *English*."

"English breakfast?" Mia reached into the cabinet and produced two boxes of tea bags. "That's a good one. I have chamomile and peppermint. Either of those sound all right?"

Zoe gave a shrug, her oversized black T-shirt shifting around her naked thighs. "I'll have whatever you're having."

"Okay. Well, I'm sort of hooked on chamomile. It's supposed to ease insomnia. I'll make you some."

Within ten minutes the two women were perched on the old counter, making small talk about tea versus coffee while their drinks steeped. Mia learned that Zoe adored caffeine in heavy doses and big sizes with lots of sugary syrups for added flavor. Zoe divulged that an eager-to-please staffer at the rehab center had bent the rules and made regular coffee runs for the actress. An alarm bell triggered at this bit of information. What other rules had been broken on the celebrity's behalf? Mia made a mental note to inquire about this later. In the spirit of sharing, Mia told her she'd had trouble sleeping and making hot tea seemed to ease her nerves at night. Zoe seemed to like this idea and nodded enthusiastically.

"It's pretty good," she said. "Better than I imagined." She took an audible slurp and giggled. "Who knew I'd like tea?"

"You said your mom did," Mia ventured cautiously. "Do you see her very much?"

"Oh, not really. She lives in France." Zoe's eyes cast toward the ground.

"Wow, that sounds cool." Mia didn't really know if it was

or not, but she was trying to remain casual. "Has she always lived there?"

"I guess it's cool." Zoe trailed off for a second. "She moved there with some artist a few years ago. I don't know. I don't talk to her very much. She's sort of the opposite of me." Mia wasn't sure what this meant, but the distance between mother and daughter was crystal clear. She decided not to probe any further for now. Even she could see that this was a tender subject for Zoe.

When the tea was done and the women had traded enough conversation for two strangers on their first meeting, Mia wished Zoe a good night and excused herself. She actually felt much more relaxed at learning there wasn't a lunatic or melodramatic oddball living in her house. Zoe sprung off the counter, thanked her host, and wandered back to her room. Back in the sanctuary of her bedroom, Mia drowsily crawled beneath the twist of covers and succumbed to a deep and dreamless slumber.

The next morning Mia awakened to the unceremonious clanging of pots and pans. She dashed out her door with a quickening pulse, afraid of discovering an intruder. What she found, after wiping the sleep from her eyes, was just as startling. There, in the middle of her kitchen, was a kimono-clad Zoe, her long hair bound in a taut bun, her small hands making hummingbird-quick chopping motions over a plate full of velvety-brown mushrooms. Broken eggshells lay scattered along the counter between puddles of spilled milk and clumps of shredded cheese. It looked as though a miniature Godzilla had stalked about the kitchen, destroying breakfast food in its wake. A pleasant scent of something promising floated in her direction, causing her stomach to stir.

Mia cleared her throat. "Hey!" Zoe jumped at the interruption and wiped her forehead with her wrist, bits of mushroom hanging from her fingers. "Surprise! I'm making breakfast," she said. "You do like breakfast, I hope." Beaming, she waited with an eager grin, her crooked tooth peeking out.

"Wow," Mia said, coming more into the room. "Sure, I love breakfast. But where did you . . ."

"Get all this food? I walked down to the market. Did you know how many people are at the store so early in the morning? It's crazy." Her sincerity was so real that Mia didn't have the heart to tell her that's what most regular people do—get up and start their day well before her usual preferred time of midafternoon.

"Glad you found the market."

"Yeah, I used the map on my phone."

"I didn't know you cooked." Mia glanced at the stove and noticed steamy white puffs of air rising from the reddened burner.

"Well, they taught us how to make omelets in rehab. It's actually pretty therapeutic. That's kind of all I know how to make," she said. "Omelets and grilled cheese."

A thought suddenly occurred to Mia. "Didn't people recognize you at the store?" Letting the neighborhood know that tabloid fodder was living nearby probably wasn't such a good idea. Plus, the house already had one potential superfan leaving drawings at the door. She didn't need more crazed admirers ringing the bell asking to meet the famous Zoe Winter. Visions of paparazzi mobs flashed in her head. A stab of panic struck at her chest.

"It's okay," Zoe said, sensing her nervousness. "I wore a hat real low and didn't have any makeup on. Most people are expecting actresses to be all done up all the time. Going grunge throws them off." She smiled and went back to her chopping.

Her fortitude was refreshing to Mia. Somehow the shy creature that had arrived at her doorstep earlier in the week had now morphed into a rather lively person. Leaning against the aged refrigerator, she examined the mystery of it all. Mia realized she'd quite possibly made all the wrong assumptions about her guest. Who was this girl, really? Perhaps she was just a normal kid who'd lost her way and had no one to guide her back. Maybe she wasn't as dark and brooding as she'd originally seemed. Standing there, watching Zoe whisk and gather up ingredients into the fry pan, Mia planned to find out more.

NINE

⁓

*M*ia stood alone in the living room. Faint car
noises and the sounds of playing children
drifted through a cracked window. The Santa
Anas had produced their final blast and mercifully moved on
down the coast, taking all of their creaky interruptions with
them.

Mia had hovered in the front room earlier as Carson and
that snappy agent, Sharon, arrived unannounced and snatched
Zoe away for a cast meeting. Zoe must have known she was
required to work that morning. Thus the early breakfast and
wide-awake attitude. But Mia found it odd that her companion hadn't mentioned it over omelets. She'd merely wiped
down the counters, mumbled something about doing the
dishes later, and excused herself. Forty-five minutes later, she
appeared freshly showered wearing a cropped knit sweater
and skinny jeans to answer the brusque knocking at the front
door. Carson and the woman handler entered with brief
hellos and a quick once-over of their client. Then the three
of them dashed away in a black Suburban, their departure
leaving Mia oddly abandoned.

Work, Mia told herself. *Get some work done.* Plodding upstairs, she made her way toward her office to sit and write. This was no easy feat. Recently, Mia was plagued by dread, even anxiety, over the need to create something new. She knew she wanted to write, but was often afraid she'd sit down and come up empty. This dread was a terrible burden to carry; it could be heavy and counterproductive, like lugging a ship's anchor through deep sand. She never fully wanted to admit this aloud, fearing she'd seal her fate and never be able to pen a second manuscript. She'd already had one failure with *Beautiful*. One mistake could be tolerated, lesson learned. But a second attempt didn't have such allowances. This next time around she needed to triumph on some level. Because of this, Mia remained resolute.

But today, in the empty hallway, Mia encountered just the kind of distraction that had the potential to stall her work. She arrived at the guest room and hesitated. Zoe's bedroom door was closed, securing all behind it to secrecy. This only allowed all kinds of images to play out in Mia's imagination. The temptation to spy on the girl twisted around inside Mia's middle, as though something important had been left undone. Dare she go inside? Would it hurt anyone if she just took a peek? Even though it was her house, Mia felt like a trespasser, hoping not to get caught among someone else's things. Reaching out with an unsteady hand, she turned the knob and nudged the door with her toe. The action produced a low creak. Without entering, she craned her neck and peered inside. Nothing to see from this vantage but crumpled bedsheets and a wet towel flung on the floor.

Nervously, she edged a little farther into the room and the aroma of spices and vanilla instantly filled her nostrils. She noted one of Emma's votive candles and a box of matches resting on the bedside table. Bending down, she instinctually picked up the discarded towel and brought it to her nose. It smelled of high-end salon shampoo. She unclenched her fingers and released it then, realizing any tidying up would divulge her snooping.

Scattered throughout the room were more clues to Zoe's life: a partially opened duffle bag, rumpled sweaters and shirts spilled outward, a coverless book upside down on the floor, the light left on in the bathroom. Mia wondered if the partially filled bag meant that Zoe hadn't wanted to unpack, if she considered her stay temporary and was anxious to leave. Mia was surprised to find herself disappointed at this thought. After all, she'd been very much against having a renter in the first place, especially such a controversial one. But now, standing in the middle of all of Zoe's things, she felt a longing for the girl to stay. *How strange*, Mia thought as she backed out of the room and eased the door shut.

A million questions skipped through Mia's head. How long would Zoe stay? Would she be able to remain sober under the pressure of work? What was that book on the floor? Could she expect another midnight conversation over tea?

Clicking on her computer, Mia waited for the screen to illuminate. Before the cursor blinked back its greeting, she opened up a new document and began pounding at the keyboard. She worked fast. Words filled the screen, like a rapid chain of black ants marching across the snow. A rush of creativity made its way to her nimble fingertips, images and scenes flying out before Mia could discern their meaning. Free flow was Mia's best kind of writing, the kind that's all imagination and zero editing. Reaching across her desk, she snatched up a loose hair band and pulled a clump of bothersome locks from her face. At times like this, distractions could not be tolerated. Leaning farther into the screen with a sharp squint, she continued her uninhibited pounding and let a little cackle escape. She was writing again.

As the hours ticked away, the room became darkened, save for an outside streetlight and the dim glow of the computer screen. Mia slumped back in her chair and shook out her weary fingers. What time was it? Had she lost all track? The only break she'd taken from her desk that day was for a quick snack of tea and a cheese sandwich. Then she was back to work again. At some point, her cell phone had broken her focus, its chirping ring only serving as an unwanted annoyance. So she had switched it to mute hours earlier.

Nestled in the home's cozy hideaway, Mia was filled with gratitude for its solace. She yawned and stretched. Her lower backed throbbed with a dull ache, but it was the good kind of ache that came from a satisfying day of long, hard work. She just knew if she hunkered down in the spot where Bradbury had squirreled away and wrote, she'd find her much-needed inspiration. She closed her eyes and tried to picture him in that very room. She imagined the generous, shaggy white hair and large, dark-rimmed eyeglasses, a prominent nose pointing stalwartly toward the pages of a typewriter. There would have been mountains of manuscript pages at his feet, coupled with photos and other illustrated works. He was known to hold on to every knickknack and gift, never wanting to part with any reminder of his creative life. She'd once read an interview where he was quoted as saying that a "writer's past was the most important thing he has." He went on to say that sometimes an object—a mask, a ticket stub—helped him remember whole experiences and out of that could come ideas for his stories.

Mia could almost detect faded marks along the beadboard walls, where many of these keepsakes had surely accumulated. Even in her imagined memory, Mia could feel these items in the room with her, keeping her company throughout the lonesome night.

But was the spirit of Bradbury the only reason for Mia's sudden burst of inspiration? Mia thought of Zoe's room, all of her belongings calling out their own story from their cast-off places. Were these things possibly a source of her stimulus? She hadn't felt alive like this, urgently filled with creativity, for a very long time. Too long. *Don't overthink it,* she told herself. *Just be grateful.*

Viewing the computer monitor, she noticed the e-mail icon flashing through the darkness like a lighthouse in a misty harbor. It was warning of something imminent. Mia could sense it. Opening her in-box, she was met with several messages from Emma and one from her father.

Since her parents had decided to escape the high prices of Southern California a couple of years earlier, and follow their friends to a retirement village in Florida, Mia had missed their presence. While she was growing up, Jim and Trudy Gladwell had been fairly hands-off when it came to their daughters' endeavors. Being ex-hippies, running a successful gourmet grocery shop that sold things like organic cauliflower, free-range chicken, and vegan soba noodle dinners, they lived a beachy Southern California lifestyle that included alternative choices and sustainable ideals. They believed children should figure out their own destiny without too much authority or institution imposed on them. As long as Emma and Mia took their education seriously, their parents gave them fairly free rein to follow their dreams. It was a parenting philosophy that Mia would forever cherish, but Emma would endlessly be trying to make up for.

Wondering what her father had to say, Mia decided to open his e-mail first: *Loved the photo of your house. That Bradbury fellow would surely be happy that another artist has inhabited his home. We are off to Sanibel Island for the weekend. Much love, Dad.*

Mia was proud of the fact that her technology-challenged father had embraced electronic correspondence so well. Her heart swelled at his encouragement. Forever the hippie, Dad always loved the idea of having an "artist" in the family. Her lackluster magazine articles were hardly art these days, but she'd take all of his compliments nonetheless. Mia had believed that she'd always reflected more of her dad's spirit than her mother's. Jim Gladwell, with his graying brown hair and unruly eyebrows, had always embraced art on such an endearing level. While he wasn't an artist himself, save for his colorful produce displays and quirky banners at the family grocery store, her dad was the one in the family who would linger the longest during a museum visit or who could be found closing his eyes and gently rocking side-to-side when listening to music. He was the one who rose every morning, excited to find the newspaper folded on his front steps, and spend time with the editorials over breakfast. Mia would like to think her drive for creativity stemmed from her father's influence. She'd leave her mother's adoration for organizing and plan making to Emma any day of the week.

As usual, several of the following e-mails were from her agenda-loving sister. Begrudgingly, Mia clicked on the first message from Emma.

Call me.

The next.

I've left you a voice mail. Where are you?

The last two were more of the same. Only the last sentence wedged an uncomfortable lump in her throat.

Seriously, answer your phone. My friend wants to photograph your house and she's very interested in having Zoe be part of the shoot. Call me ASAP.

Damn you, Emma! She wasn't supposed to let anyone know about Zoe living in the house. It was one thing for Emma's country club friends to feign interest in the house and its history, but it was another matter entirely for Zoe's presence to be announced. This was going to cause a problem. She was sure of it. Time to call Carson.

TEN

~

*M*ia sat and stewed in the dim room. Carson's phone had gone straight to voice mail, so she opted not to leave a message. What would she even say? Instead, she paced around on the rug and cursed her sister and her intrusive friends. She also cursed Carson for putting her in such a bind. On top of all of this, festering under her skin was the fact that it was nearing 8:00 p.m. and there was still no sign of Zoe. Shouldn't the girl check in? Mia was her so-called babysitter after all. Is this what she was to expect every evening? It was not lost on her that this was perhaps how parents of teenagers often felt.

As if on cue, the doorbell rang, followed by a faint knocking. Taking the stairs in twos, Mia bounded to the entry and flung open the door. Her cheeks turned a dark shade of pink as she met Zoe's eyes. She didn't want to reveal her foolish concern.

"Sorry. I don't have a key." Zoe slunk through the doorway. To Mia's relief, she was sober and intact.

"I'll see if I can find a spare." Mia followed Zoe into the breakfast room and watched her plunk a hefty purse onto the floor. It appeared stuffed to the gills. Did she have clothes in there? *A girl always on the run,* thought Mia.

"And this was on your door," Zoe said. Reaching out, her hand uncurled to bare a partially folded square of paper. Another sketch. "I didn't read it," Zoe offered, slightly defensive.

"That's okay." Mia snatched the paper up and stuffed it in her pocket. She avoided Zoe's stare. Although curiosity burned through her like a searing hole, she preferred to discover the contents in private. Mia wasn't ready to disclose that a stranger had been leaving drawings ever since she'd moved in. It would surely scare off most people, let alone a guarded actress. Mia wasn't sure if she should be scared herself. But somehow she suspected the notes were meant as a friendly gesture. From whom, she didn't have a clue, but for now, she was committed to unraveling the mystery alone.

"Hello? Anybody here?" Carson bellowed from the front hallway.

"We're in here," Mia answered. She glanced at Zoe, who reminded her of a drooping flower the way she was collapsing into a chair. The color and life Mia noticed in Zoe that morning were now faded and far away. She hadn't realized until that moment how tired the girl was. "Tea?"

Zoe rubbed her forehead with the heel of her hand and nodded. "Please." Mia went to work getting the kettle going. Striding in, Carson greeted his women.

His voice felt too big for the room. "How is everyone?"

He paused next to Mia and wrapped a strong arm around her shoulder. His button-down shirt was rolled up at the elbows, revealing the golden tan of his skin. Cedar goodness enveloped Mia. The warmth of him was intoxicating. For an instant she had the inclination to lean in, but she shook off the thought and busied herself with Zoe's drink instead.

"Fine." Mia met his eye. "That was an awfully long first day of work." *Especially for someone who's been recuperating in rehab for the past several months.* Like a disapproving parent, she wanted to express this sentiment aloud to Carson. But hoping to spare Zoe, she stuffed the idea back down.

"Oh, Zoe here's young. She's got more vigor in her little finger than you and I have in our whole being. Isn't that right, Zoe?" Carson waved his arms in a large sweep, like someone giving a toast. His ignorance of the situation made Mia fume. The intoxicating magic he had brought into the room had now evaporated. Was he really this inept at reading women? She didn't know Zoe well, but anyone could tell by the girl's weary expression that the day had drained her.

Carson propped himself against the counter and carelessly crossed his loafered feet. "Besides, she's got you to look after her." He aimed his complacency at Mia now.

"Uh-huh." The kettle let out a high whistle, a jet of white steam shooting out. Mia floated a bag of chamomile in Zoe's mug. "Can I talk to you for a minute?" She glared at her ex and tilted a chin toward the living room. Still oblivious, Carson shrugged and followed her.

"Come upstairs with me."

"Oh, sounds promising," he whispered and nudged her ribs.

Mia rolled her eyes at him. "Oh my god, Carson," she said. "Get a grip." Yanking him by the sleeve, she led him to the upper level and through the doors of her study.

"Wow, you never let me into your precious office area." His eyes slowly took in the room, and came to rest on the blinking computer screen. "You've been working?" Without waiting for an answer, he roamed her office space, stopping to peer at her college books on the shelves and then picking up a framed article and photo of Bradbury. "This is the same room," he said, pointing as if it were a new discovery. It was as if he was just putting together the fact that Mia's idol had once been in that very house.

"No kidding, Sherlock." Mia snatched the silver frame from his hand and carefully replaced it. "You really are a child sometimes, aren't you?" To prove her point, he plopped down in her chair and kicked his feet on her desk, his grin reaching both ears.

"You'll never let me sit at your beloved desk again, so I better do it while I can," he said in mock defiance. Just as she started to protest, he clutched her arm and pulled her to his lap.

Carson knew how to play his women well. Mia was no exception. When he saw a scolding coming, he usually headed it off with some playful flirtation. As irritated as Mia was, she weakened just a bit. Carson would always be Carson. He looked at her then, their eyes catching for just a moment, their faces inches apart. The warmth of him surrounded her and she remembered how he used to hold her, how they used to lie in bed at night and wrap their limbs around one another and talk about anything and everything for hours. They used to be so good together. It was all good until it was not.

Sensing her hesitation, Carson opened his lips as if to speak. But Mia wasn't ready to let her guard down so easily. She rose abruptly and dismissed the intimacy. A small glimmer of light left Carson's eyes, as he watched her move away from him. It was a pained look that Mia knew well.

Not willing to give in to the distraction, she turned to face him. "Don't you see that Zoe is vulnerable right now? She just came out of her cave of solitude last night and then she's snatched up and made to perform like a dancing monkey. Didn't you notice her out there? She's exhausted!" Her whole body went rigid as she gestured downstairs. "I think all of this is too soon."

Now it was Carson who was on his feet, sending her swivel chair rolling backward, as he bore down on her with his tone. "Too soon? Too soon?" He was incredulous. "Mia, if anything it's almost too late. This girl has been under contract for a long time and the studio stood around with its dick in its hand waiting for her to sober up."

"I realize—"

"No, you don't realize, Mia." He was pacing now, his pant legs making swift swishing sounds as he moved. It was rare to witness Carson worry outwardly. Maybe she'd come at him too severely. "You barely know this girl. Why are you all of a sudden so concerned?"

Mia nodded. "You're right, I barely know her. But when she came into this house she was a frightened child. In just the past twenty-four hours she was courageous enough to come out of her shell only to be whisked away to Holly-woodland again. My gut says she's not ready, that's all."

"*Hollywoodland* is where she works. It's where I work. It's what's paying for all of our rents, including yours, Mia!" He was yelling now, his anger boiling over.

"I realize that." Mia's arms folded tight across her chest. There it was. Carson was holding the house over her head like an enormous debt that could never be collected.

After a beat he softened a bit. "Why do you care all of a sudden? I thought you'd be happy to have her out of your hair."

"I don't know," she said. "I just like her." It dawned on Mia that she really did like this girl. There was something about her cautious smile, her weariness of the world, her attitude of hopefulness despite it all that Mia admired. From the moment Zoe had stepped across her threshold, Mia had some profound urge to protect this young girl. For lack of a better description, Mia guessed this was what it felt like to be maternal.

SEVERAL DAYS DRIFTED BY AND ZOE AND MIA SETTLED into a regular routine. The two would usually meet up during the late hours of the night, both unable to settle into sleep, opting for tea and company instead. What followed was usually a fitful night for Mia, images of the mysterious drawings skipping across her dreams like swift stones on an unsteady river. And while Zoe didn't repeat her extravagant omelet breakfasts, she would arise early and leave small gestures for her host. One morning Mia stumbled into the kitchen to find a newly purchased box of green tea next to a Post-it note of a smiley face. Another morning she discovered all of the previous night's dishes had been washed and carefully set back in the cupboards. At each new discovery Mia was surprised at Zoe's generous spirit.

Something about these small exchanges set Mia's inspiration on high. Once Zoe had gone to work for the day, Mia would race up to her study and bang out a couple of thousand words of writing. It was invigorating to be creating again. Usually this kind of work required outlines and character studies and tedious synopses, but now she merely sat down and words began spilling forth like a hose that had finally been unkinked. She didn't know how long the inspiration was going to last, but she didn't care. The feeling was thrilling.

It was during one of these illuminating sessions that an interruption came at the front door. Although it was only noon and too early for Zoe to be home, Mia rubbed at her computer-blurred vision and ambled downstairs, assuming her tenant had forgotten the extra key again. To her disdain, the person on the other side of the door was not Zoe but an agitated Emma.

"Oh, it's you," Mia stumbled backward at the discovery, fighting the instinct to flee.

Emma hovered before her in her tailored suit and designer heels, as she gave her sister the once-over. Her reaction was that of a put-upon stylist forced to work with a known slob. Mia shifted from one slippered foot to another, realizing she hadn't bothered to brush her hair or teeth yet. One of the benefits of being a writer was the ability to show up for work in your pajamas. By Emma's expression, she might have at least made an effort to clean up.

"Yes, it's me," Emma said, pushing past her. "So sorry to disappoint. Who did you think you were going to greet in your robe?"

Mia sighed audibly. This was not the kind of day she'd planned to have. "Well come on in, why don't you?" She slammed the door just a little too loud.

"Mia, what's going on with you? I've been leaving messages for days. Didn't you get them?" Emma crossed her arms like a scolding schoolteacher.

Mia tried to meet her sister's eye. "Yes, I've just been busy, that's all."

"Busy doing what, exactly? Looks to me like you've just been lounging your days away." Emma surveyed the front room, her gaze resting on an empty mug and dirty plate alongside a stack of papers. "Are you depressed?"

"Geez, Emma. No, I'm not depressed. I'm working." Mia was being examined like a specimen in a lab. She didn't like this kind of scrutiny, especially in her own home. But Emma had been scrutinizing her since childhood, so what was the difference now?

Emma raised an eyebrow, peering closer. "Really? What are you working on?"

"I don't know yet." Mia wanted to shrink back into herself. She wasn't ready to discuss what she'd been writing.

The truth was she didn't want to jinx the streak of creativity that had been floating around her like a cloud of good luck. For the past week, she'd been writing with wild abandon. But deep down, she worried the spark might flicker out as quickly as it had been lit. There was no telling how much time she had to get the ideas out.

"What do you mean you don't know?"

Something inside Mia snapped, like an arm that had been bent one too many times. "Oh, Emma just give it a rest! I'm working and that's all you need to know!" Mia braced herself. Neither of them spoke, leaving the room awkwardly still with only the murmur of street sounds in the background. The clock ticked on the mantle. No one moved. Blood rushed into Mia's ears as they both teetered on the edge of what would surely become a fight.

Forming her lips into a tight pucker, Emma spoke first. "Fine, then. Let's talk about something more pressing." Her return was icy. If she was stung by her younger sister, she wasn't about to show it. "How is Zoe adjusting?"

"How's she adjusting? Like from rehab?"

This time it was Emma who would let out a forced sigh. This game of back and forth was a pure waste of her time. "Is the guest room in disarray or can it be tidied up for a photo shoot?" There it was; that was all she cared about. It wasn't the well-being of Zoe that she was after; it was the matter of using the house and its present situation to her own advantage.

Mia swallowed hard. She'd forgotten about Emma and her inconvenient decorator friend. Maybe she hadn't totally forgotten, more like pushed the thought into a dark compartment and shut it tight until a later date. How was she going to get around this one?

"Emma, no one is supposed to know that Zoe is here. I thought you were aware of that."

"Well, only Jeannie knows, and I had to let it slip because she was asking about coming back to shoot the staging job and you weren't answering your phone and well, what else was I to say?" Emma was almost panting, working herself into a froth.

"Easy. You just say, 'Gee Jeannie, now's not really a good time.' End of story." Mia thrust her fury into neatening up the room, collecting the dishes into her arms and tossing stray pillows back onto the couch. "Carson is trusting me to handle this, so I'd appreciate you not blowing it for me." She stormed toward the kitchen with her precarious load.

"I told you that tying yourself to Carson was a bad idea, and now look at the mess he's gotten you into." Emma scurried behind her, clucking like an agitated wren. "Nothing good has ever come from this relationship, Mia. Now you're hooked for life!"

Mia whirled around too hastily; the stray plate escaped her grasp and crashed to the floor. "Damn it!" She dropped to her knees, hoping to sweep the bits of porcelain into her hands. Salty tears sprung out of nowhere and threatened to run down her enflamed cheeks.

Cradling pieces of the plate in her hand, she tried to clear her blurred vision with her forearm. With a quivering chin, she gathered up her breath only to let a sob escape as she turned to face her hovering sister. "I'm grateful to Carson for what he did. You may never understand our friendship, and I don't care. Zoe is his client and I'm trying to protect her from too much. You coming here demanding answers is *too much*. Don't you get that?" Sinking farther onto the wooden floorboards, she made one violent sweep of her hand and gathered the shards of plate. She was too angry to bother about the fact that her actions had now drawn blood.

"I'm sorry, I didn't mean to get you so upset." Emma's speech relaxed. Crouching down, she took Mia's arm and eased her back onto her feet. "Let's get you into the kitchen and find a Band-Aid." With all of her motherly gentleness, Emma helped Mia to hold her bleeding hand over the sink and told her to hold tight while she went in search of first aid supplies from Mia's bathroom.

A few minutes later, she returned with a box of bandages and carefully wrapped Mia's hand. "Well, that's quite the vanity," she said of the master en suite. "Mrs. Bradbury must have been pleased with her bathroom, don't you think?" Despite it all, Emma was trying. Mia knew Emma's interest in the Brad-burys was slight, but nonetheless she appreciated the effort.

"Isn't it sweet? I love all the mirrors," Mia said. "If I paid more attention to my hair and makeup, that would be a real treat." The two both giggled at this. Primping was Emma's occupation, not Mia's.

When they were done laughing over the irony, the two leaned against the sink and regarded one another. It was Emma who offered the first concession. "I can hold Jeannie off for a while."

"Are you sure?" Relief wafted over Mia's whole body.

"I'm sure," she said. Emma looked at her watch and righted herself. "I've got to run, but come by the house soon. The kids miss you." With that, she clip-clopped her way to the entry and said good-bye with a little wave.

"Emma?" Mia said just as her sister disappeared.

"Yes?" Emma's head poked back around the corner.

"Thank you."

ELEVEN

*I*t was the weekend, and Mia opted to rise with the sun and head out for a hike. She hadn't had much free time to roam the neighborhood and check out all of its historical architecture. Plus it had been too long since she'd really exercised, and camping out at her desk every day, whittling away at her stash of chocolate, had done nothing for her thickening middle. The weather was mild and the terrain was just enough of an incline to give her the workout she so badly craved. Cutting through a well-maintained neighborhood greenbelt, she greeted other walkers who bounced balls for their dogs and stretched before starting their runs. It wasn't a busy area by any means, but it revived Mia to be around other human life. Zoe was at work much of the time, and Mia had holed herself up in her office for hours on end. It was nice to get out of her head for once and soak up some nature.

On her return home, she strolled by a particularly impressive rose garden that bordered a Spanish-style home. It cheered her to come across such vivid hues, their perfume beckoning her closer. Although it was November, she decided she would make a plan for her own backyard. A rose garden seemed like a nice addition. She decided she'd go home and spend some time in the yard during the weekend.

Dashing up the front steps, she returned home and listened for any signs of life. All was still and tomblike. Zoe must have been taking advantage of her day off by catching up on sleep. Mia had had little contact with Zoe lately. She'd often wondered what the girl's day was like once the black SUV had zoomed her away to some unknown studio for read-throughs and costume fittings. It was only in the late hours of the night that Zoe would wearily enter the house and mutter a tired hello. She'd mention something about cast dinners or spending time with the director. She always appeared sober to Mia's watchful observation, but a part of Mia still worried that such a heavy schedule might not be the best thing for a girl just finding herself again.

Kicking her sneakers off in the foyer, Mia padded on stocking feet through the house and went about making breakfast. Standing in the coolness of her refrigerator, she realized maybe she should stock the house with more substantial food. Being on her own and often eating at her computer, she lived on a steady supply of yogurts and toast with peanut butter. It wasn't that she didn't know how to cook; she actually prided herself on a few specialties like her cranberry chicken. Mia wondered if she might make dinner to share with Zoe. She'd certainly have to get more ingredients that lent themselves to the crafting of a solid meal.

Making a note, she listed a visit to the grocery store as one more thing she wanted to do that day.

It was while Mia was taking stock of her kitchen that a drowsy-eyed Zoe stumbled in. Her ever-bouncy auburn hair was fastened in a messy ponytail. Mia noticed how even in her worst hour this girl had flawless skin—like the surface of a still pond, not a ripple in sight. Sensing Mia's watchful eye, Zoe offered a smile and went about brewing her tea. It warmed Mia that her new friend had traded coffee for her favorite chamomile. Perhaps she was making an impression on the girl.

Zoe, most assuredly, was making an impression on her. She'd been up the night before going over her most recent pages, when she identified a common thread in the work. Zoe's presence seemed to exist on nearly every page. There was something so intriguing about her. This girl was the embodiment of sweetness and mystery, beauty and fragility. She was like a lovely butterfly in a busy garden that lights upon your hand only to fly away just before you make contact with the wings. Without fully realizing it, Mia had been including clear elements of Zoe into her new story. She'd spent a good portion of her sleepless night reflecting on this revelation. Not only had she recently attacked her writing with frantic energy, but she was also diving into a completely new variety of prose. Where Mia had been stuck, she was now liberated. Where she'd been fearful, she was now bold. There could only be one answer. Zoe Winter had become her muse.

"I found this," Zoe interrupted Mia's thoughts. She

waited with an outstretched hand that bared a small square of paper.

Mia started. Another drawing. In Zoe's palm sat a wolf-faced dragon creature baring a devious, toothy grin. Its legs were scratchy pencil lines accompanied by a thick, scraggly tail. The entire sketch was no bigger than a dollar bill, but its meaning was much weightier.

"Where'd you get this?" Mia asked, although she already knew.

"It was near the front door last night when I came in," Zoe said. "You were already asleep, so I couldn't ask you. It's weird, right?" Zoe shuffled into the breakfast nook with Mia right behind. The women sat down and inspected the mystery that now lay on the table between them.

"Do you know who left this?" Zoe figured it was cryptic. "It's a little haunting, isn't it?"

"Yes, I guess so." This was it. Mia was going to have to divulge the fact that some stranger was leaving odd notes at the house and it could possibly be a superfan or a crazy person who might put Zoe's living arrangements in jeopardy. How was Mia going to explain something that she could not yet explain to herself? She'd already witnessed the sour reaction that her sister gave upon discovering another note. A note in which Mia actually found a delightful resemblance to the Halloween tree.

"Well, did Carson tell you anything about this house before you moved in?" Mia ventured carefully. *Don't startle her*, she thought.

"Yeah, he said it was a famous author's house before you

bought it." Zoe blew into her tea and gave a sheepish glance. "I kinda figured that's the only reason you wanted to live in this house that's kind of, well, old." Mia couldn't tell if Zoe was impressed or embarrassed by how retro it all was.

"Yes, it's old. The house belonged to Ray Bradbury and his family. They moved into here in the 50s." She waited for Zoe's reaction. The girl said nothing as she nursed her tea, so Mia went on. "Ray Bradbury wrote a lot of iconic books. Some people call them science fiction, others say speculative fiction. It was all very futuristic, and he had a keen ability to determine what life would be like with all the advances in technology. Many of his stories were like cautionary tales."

"Like space aliens and end of the world stuff?"

"Yes and no. It wasn't like your generation's crazy dystopian movies." Mia thought for a minute. How could she explain this better? "Okay, like his book *Fahrenheit 451*. That posed the question of what would happen if people got so caught up with television and technology that they thought reading was bad and they started burning books and the houses that kept them. It was both a warning about getting too wrapped up in technology and a love letter to books. Does this make any sense?" She'd shredded it, she was sure. It was impossible to put Bradbury's work into a neat package and present it over the length it takes one to finish her drink. But something in Zoe's green eyes flickered.

"Okay, I think I get it. It's like, what if we all walked around texting too much and people suddenly thought talking was bad, so any talkers got punished?" Zoe beamed.

"Yes! That's a good analogy," Mia said. "Not all of his

books were about this, but that's the idea. I have a copy of *Fahrenheit* if you ever want to read it." Mia almost let it escape that she'd seen another book in Zoe's room, but came to her senses before leaking her betrayal.

"What's the 451 mean?"

"Oh, that's the temperature at which he believed paper burned."

"Cool." Zoe leaned in and held up the sketch. "But, what does any of that have to do with *this*?"

"Honestly, I'm not really sure," Mia ventured. "Ever since I moved in, these drawings have been showing up like tiny clues. But I don't know what they're clues to. All I know is that they remind me of different Bradbury stories. Bradbury drew a little, but he wasn't a huge illustrator. I don't know his art well enough to know if these are what he worked on or if some fan is paying homage to their favorite author or what." She collapsed back into her chair. The burden of the secret had been lifted.

Quite the opposite, Zoe sat erect in her chair. Energized by the story, she was suddenly charged, reaching her arm across the small table and slapping her palm on its surface, as though hitting a game show buzzer. "This is your Boo Radley!" she squealed.

Mia frowned. "My?"

"Boo Radley!" she repeated. "You know, like in *To Kill a Mockingbird*? I did a scene from it in my theater group and this totally reminds me of the scaredy-cat albino neighbor who leaves gifts for Scout in the tree!" Zoe inched farther forward. "I'm going to help you find your Boo Radley."

TWELVE

*W*hat if this person doesn't want to be found? Or what if he's not really as sweet and harmless as Boo Radley?" Mia didn't know whether to feel calm or frantic by Zoe's urgent push to flush this stranger out.

Zoe rose from the breakfast table and collected her mug. "I've dealt with scary fanatics before," she said in a surprisingly glib reply. "They're usually much more stalker-ish. They want to be seen and known. They'll follow you on Twitter, try to contact your agent, and even send weirdo photos of themselves. This person isn't doing any of those things."

Mia sat dumbfounded as Zoe wandered into the kitchen. "But I don't have a Twitter account and my agent has fallen off the face of the earth, and how do we know this person isn't spying on us from his car all day, waiting for his moment to pounce?" Her collection of fears came tumbling out like unsightly clutter from an overfilled closet.

Zoe poked her head back through the doorway. "Maybe you're right. But wouldn't you want to find out what you're dealing with instead of making up things in your head?" For a twenty-three-year-old, she was awfully sensible. If she only knew about the fantastical dreams Mia was having at night. "If you're really freaked out we can call my bodyguard. He could stand out front and act menacing." She came back into the room and gave her best impression of a threatening stare.

Mia chuckled, grateful for the lighthearted presence of her new friend.

The remainder of the morning consisted of the two women conspiring over how to catch their mystery artist. They spread the drawings out onto the breakfast table: the winged dragon, the wispy tree, and the obscure wolf. It wasn't until Mia examined them, all lined up like miniature character composites, that she thought to dig out the fourth drawing she'd pocketed the week before. When Zoe had originally presented her with a drawing, Mia had crammed the paper into her jeans only to become distracted by Carson. Because of the commotion with him that night, she'd forgotten all about it. Thinking of the scrap of paper now, she ran to retrieve her pants from the hamper, scolding herself for nearly allowing the sketch to be ruined in the wash. What she produced was the most curious of all four drawings.

There in the folds of a yellowed square of paper were a half dozen tiny faces. Each one was no larger than a child's marble, and they were strewn about the paper in no particular pattern. These funny little elfin faces bore extra-large eyes and ears as well as geometric-shaped noses. Some had what appeared to be a pair of alien antennae affixed to the top of their round heads. Some had plump mouths set in sober expressions, while others had no mouths at all. Mia squinted hard to pick out any detail that might give her a better clue. Nothing familiar came to mind, only that the images had a bit of resemblance to the others because of their thin pencil strokes and lack of any dimension or shading. They reminded her of a cartoonist's early drafts before he might commit to something more substantial. Showing them to Zoe, Mia only shrugged with confusion.

"What do you think they mean?" Zoe asked, her dainty swoop of a nose pressed close to the table, loose strands of auburn hair falling around her bright face. "Are they telling you a story? Maybe they're a secret code to something." Her eyes glimmered with possibility. She was totally invested.

Mia hadn't pegged her as an inquisitive person until now. She was impressed at Zoe's ability to be outside of herself, considering her age and celebrity status. Encouraged, she went on to give Zoe her best interpretation of each drawing, careful not to overwhelm her with too many literary details. It wasn't that she thought Zoe couldn't grasp the significance of the stories; it was more that she was still somewhat afraid to frighten her. Like a child, Zoe had been attracted to something colorful and shiny. But what if that object turned intensely dark and threatening? After all, they didn't really know what they were dealing with. Zoe had just come out the other end of darkness; Mia had witnessed it when she opened her home to a glum-looking girl not too long ago. A big part of Mia felt the need to keep things light and comfortable. She wanted Zoe to unpack those bags and stay awhile. Was this selfish? Mia couldn't be sure. True, she did like the effect Zoe had on her writing as of late. But more than that, she felt it her duty to offer Zoe shelter from the storm. There was more than just her work riding on her capacity to do so.

After remaining thoughtful for a bit, Mia had an idea. "We need another opinion."

"From who?"

"Let's go find my brother-in-law, Tom."

ON THIS PARTICULAR SUNDAY AFTERNOON, TOM Hutter was found atop a tall metal ladder, his top half hanging over the edge of his shingled roof. When the women pulled up to the front of the two-story colonial house, with its carefully manicured patch of lawn and polished stone walkway, the sight of Tom dangling precariously high startled Mia. She climbed out of her car and jogged up the walkway.

"Hey there, brother. What's going on?" She shielded her eyes to block out the blinding sun.

A ruffled head of light brown hair emerged, attached to a broad grinning face and clear blue eyes. "Mia! I've been instructed to clean the gutters!" He said it like he'd been honored with a noble duty.

"Emma wanted you to get up there?"

"No, Emma wanted me to pay an ungodly amount of

money for someone else to get up here. She's crazy. I can do it myself."

"I'm sure you can," Mia conceded. "Can you come down off your ladder and meet my friend?"

Mia loved Tom because he was the yin to Emma's yang. While Emma spent her days organizing school fundraisers and charity dinners, right down to the last calligraphed place setting, Tom preferred to entertain his UCLA undergrads in the backyard, always with the barbecue tongs in hand and sometimes with a Marlboro cigarette hanging from the corner of his impish mouth. Tom was the guy who made forty-five look cool to his twentysomething students. He rarely combed his hair, his shoes were often untied, and he had a short, scratchy beard that most likely annoyed his wife. But he was charming and kind and the first one up in the mornings to make peanut butter lunches for their kids before they headed off to elementary school. Also, to Mia's constant glee, he was usually in her corner when Emma had a bone to pick with her younger sister.

THIRTY MINUTES LATER, AFTER INTRODUCTIONS WERE made and Tom had won Zoe over with his charm, the three sat huddled in the backyard on blue-cushioned chairs. Amid a scattering of children's toys, they discussed their predicament over a batch of cookies. Emma and the kids were nowhere to be found, thus Tom's gleeful presentation of a plate stacked with snickerdoodles. Usually, he was banned from that shelf of the pantry. But today he tilted back in his patio chair, kicked off his flip-flops, and popped sugar into his mouth like a man returned from a shipwrecked island.

"So you're telling me you have a stalker of the literary sort?" he said, his mouth bursting with crumbs.

Mia interjected. "*Not* a stalker. Can we stop using that word?"

"Well, what would you call this person?" Tom asked.

"How about just mystery person?"

"A sketchy sketcher?"

"No."

"A creepy creeper?" Now Tom was having fun. He rocked back on the hind legs of his chair and considered the evidence.

"I think he's like a Boo Radley," Zoe said, nibbling on a cookie.

"Ah, a character from one of the greatest novels of all time," Tom said, scratching the short whiskers of his beard. "That's interesting. But remember, Boo didn't really want to be found. He only came out of hiding to save the kids in that story."

"So you're saying one of us has to be in harm's way to lure this person out of hiding? And what makes you guys think it's a man? What if it's a woman or even a kid?" Mia asked.

"What if it is?" Tom asked. "Would that make a difference?"

"I don't know. Maybe."

"Why?"

"Because a kid doesn't feel as dangerous as a fully-grown-sneaking-around kind of adult, that's why."

"I see your point."

The three of them ping-ponged ideas back and forth for a while until the front door slammed. Like schoolchildren wanting to avoid being caught by the teacher, they silenced themselves and waited for Emma's approach.

Her ever-clicking high heels announced her entrance. She could be heard through the screen door, walking the perimeter of the house, stopping to listen, and then calling out for her husband.

"We're out here!" Tom shouted back. He shoved the plate full of cookies in Zoe's direction and gave her a quick wink.

Emma emerged through the screen in a pressed linen shirt and dark jeans. Her hair was a flawless cascade of loose curls and her lips shone with a thick layer of gloss. Even on a lazy Sunday afternoon she was buttoned up.

"Well, what a surprise," Emma said, sliding back the patio door and surveying the scene. Glancing from her husband to her sister and then taking in the image of Zoe Winter in her backyard, she looked a little wounded, like someone who hadn't been invited to the party. Covering up her bruised feelings, she stepped up to Zoe and extended a manicured hand. "How do you do? You must be Zoe."

Zoe pushed up from her chair and shook Emma's hand. "Yeah, hi. Nice to meet you. You have a beautiful house."

Emma gripped Zoe's hand for a long pause, raking her eyes over her size 0 denim shorts, her flowing hair that brushed across porcelain-skinned shoulders, and her injection-free pout. Emma drank in every ounce of Zoe's beauty. It was like witnessing a vampire quiver at the sight of fresh young blood, intoxicated and covetous all at the same time.

"Ahem!" Mia interrupted her sister's trance. "Where are the kids?"

"Oh," Emma said, regaining her composure and dropping Zoe's hand. "Michael is at soccer practice and Anna's with a friend."

"Shoot, I wanted to see them." Mia missed hugging her nephew and niece, the way they smelled of Goldfish crackers and fruit juice. Being around the kids always felt like being in the presence of uncomplicated joy.

"Well, you might want to call ahead next time so we can all plan to be here." Emma emphasized the last part, accusing Mia with her tone.

"Zoe and I were just running errands and thought we'd take a shot." She avoided Emma's suspicious gaze and pretended to busy herself with brushing cookie crumbs from the table.

"What am I, chopped liver?" Tom feigned offense.

"Of course not, Tom. Don't be silly," Emma scolded. "It's just that Mia doesn't come by very often, and when she does decide to grace us with her presence, it'd be nice to be made aware. And by the way, husband, you're not fooling anyone with those cookies." Tom's mouth popped open in retort, but he thought better of it and said nothing.

Having had enough verbal berating for one afternoon, Mia gestured to Zoe and the two of them began their swift exit. Mia hugged Emma and promised to call next time. Sensing tension, Zoe scooted through the house and headed for the door.

"Well, she's something, isn't she?" Emma whispered into Mia's ear at the end of their embrace.

"Yes, she is," Mia said. "Give the kids a squeeze from me, okay?"

"Let me know how things progress!" Tom called after Mia as she made her escape.

"What things?" Emma could be heard asking.

"Oh, writing stuff," he replied. Mia breathed a relieved sigh and carefully shut the door behind her.

THIRTEEN

⁓

*M*onday morning, Mia had a plan. It seemed to her that the mystery artist was in the habit of leaving his or her sketches early in the morning or late at night. While she couldn't lurk outside her house all of the time, she could increase the odds of intercepting the next delivery. So she set the alarm for 5:00 a.m. and convinced herself that waking at dawn would serve a double purpose; she could get outdoors and meet her neglected exercise quota and could also be on the lookout for any suspicious characters in the vicinity. It was the best she could do, short of Zoe's suggestion of writing a Dear Anonymous letter and posting it to her door. That seemed too strange, so she opted for the more sensible plan instead.

Daylight savings had turned the mornings dark and cold, making it less inviting to abandon the cozy quilted layers of her bed to strap on her running shoes. Telling herself that it was for the best, she went ahead with it anyway.

Once outside, she warmed up her muscles and took in

the length of her sleepy street. The Spanish bungalows and remodeled colonials all appeared as if in slumber, their shades pulled taut like shut eyelids. Front lawns glistened with dew; across the street sprinklers hissed to life, spitting their spray in robotic movements. Songbirds collected high above her in a tall elm, just beginning their first chirps of the morning. The air was damp and fresh, and it felt good to take in large gulps of the new day. While Mia bent over to tighten a shoelace, a solitary gray cat emerged from a nearby bush, coming over to mew and curl itself around her standing leg.

With a free hand, Mia scratched behind its triangular ears, producing a soft purr. "Why, hello there, Mister Cat," she cooed. "It appears you and I are the only ones awake this morning." The cat purred louder and continued to wind around her ankles. It wore a red collar, but no tag showing a name or address. Although the cat was small, she figured it was well fed and merely out for a morning prowl for curiosity's sake. She continued to indulge her feline companion a minute longer, while she surveyed the street once more. Not noticing any other activity, she said good-bye and followed the sidewalk, making note of the houses nearest her address.

A pink line of sunlight was pushing its way above the horizon, its ribbon of light growing broader by the minute. Accelerating her pace, she rounded the corner, swinging her arms as she went. Her breath was now coming as quick as her steps. This is what Mia loved. Walking. She'd always been a walker. She could go for hours. Hiking the foothills or strolling along the coastline were usually her favorite places to do this. Running was never for her. The world would go by in a blur when she ran, the colors and shapes melding together. No, she didn't care for that at all. She preferred to take in her surroundings, to study the landscape and observe the people and pets that crossed her path. Each of these observations was recorded in her mental catalog, stored away for when she needed to recall it in her writing. A good setting required inspiration, something to draw from, and these walks were the best resource she could imagine.

Lengthening her stride, she moved down the next street and kept her eyes peeled for suspicious persons. After a time, she let the movement take over. With each step her thoughts began to clear. She sucked air deep into her lungs and let it fill her body, sweeping away the cobwebs that clung to the corners of her mind. Pumping her arms and moving at a rapid clip made her feel capable, and this was a feeling that she wanted to hold on to all day. After a while, she forgot entirely about spying on her neighbors.

On a high from her outing, her face flushed and feet properly wearied, Mia navigated her way back to her block. Approaching the bright yellow house, its radiance greeting her like a spring flower, she noticed someone or something moving in the opposite direction of her driveway. Pressing into a jog, she narrowed her eyelids into focus and zeroed in on a man in a dark jacket and slacks making his way across the street and up a row of houses. Either his pace was quickening or Mia's was slowing, because she couldn't quite close the gap between them. He was a good hundred yards ahead of her. Should she call out? What would she say? Mia wasn't sure if the man had been leaving her driveway or not;

he could have just been coming from somewhere else. But why, at such an early hour of the morning, would someone be loitering around a house other than his own? Or maybe he wasn't loitering. Maybe Mia was on such high alert for suspicious behavior that her eyes were playing tricks on her.

Without thinking it through, she yelled out, "Hey!" The figure continued to move away from her. The gap was widening. She forced her jog into a sprint, her feet pounding the pavement, blood pumping in her ears. With a final effort, she cupped a hand around her mouth and called once more, "Hey, there!" In her haste to catch up, Mia neglected to pay attention to her footing, ignoring the fractured sidewalk's jagged surface. The toe of her sneaker caught on the edge of a tree root. In an instant she was airborne, like a splayed bird. All time and space froze for a terrifying instant. She came down hard with a skid, her palms scraped, her knee bloodied. Searing pain gripped her instantly, shooting through her limbs and striking her immobile. Through a blur of tears and snot, Mia lifted her head and scanned the street. Her mystery man had vanished.

"WHAT HAPPENED TO YOU?" ZOE STOOD OVER MIA'S chair in horror. "Are you all right?"

Mia pressed a bag of frozen broccoli to her now swelling knee and sniffed. A thick streak of blood trickled down from her wound like a tiny river, pooling into the ankle of her sock. "Ouch. Not really." It had taken all of her energy to climb the steps and plunk herself down at the kitchen table.

Ashamed, she sat nursing her injuries like an old woman. "I thought I saw him out there, so I started to run, but he was too far away and my running's not so good and, oh, I don't even know what I saw."

"You're rambling a little bit," Zoe said. "Did you hit your head?" She put a cool palm to Mia's sticky forehead. Its gentleness made Mia want to shut her eyes.

"No, I just banged up my knee."

"Are you sure, because one time my friend Parker hit his head doing skateboard tricks and he kept repeating himself until someone finally drove him to the hospital."

"I'm fine, really." Mia felt stupid sitting there answering her.

"Okay, well, what did you see exactly?"

Mia scooted her chair back and attempted to bring her leg up on the table. "Yeow!" She placed it back onto the chair, resting her hand gingerly on the frozen vegetables. "I was coming up the street when I could have sworn I saw a man leaving the house. But I was kind of far away and he could have just been walking past the house, really. I just don't know."

"What did he look like?" Zoe pulled up a chair and sat down.

"That's just it; I have no idea. I only saw the back of his head. It was dark blond or light brown, I guess. Sandy colored. He had on a jacket and slacks, like someone going to work. Who knows?"

Zoe pulled on a section of her shiny hair and coiled it around a finger. "Hmmm. Mysterious male prowling around the house. Interesting."

"You're still on your Boo kick, aren't you?"

"Maybe."

"Well, I put myself in harm's way, so to speak. I was lying flat out on the sidewalk with the wind knocked out of me and our mystery person didn't come save me. So, you might want to rethink your theory." Mia didn't intend for her words to have as much bite as they did, but watching her pulsing knee turn into a dark shade of blue wasn't helping her mood. "I truly think this person is just a fan paying tribute to his idol. People probably assume that his family still owns the house. Not too many people know we're here."

Zoe frowned. "So then how do you explain that guy you just saw? Was he the fan? Did he look like a science fiction nut?"

Mia straightened. "Do I look like a science fiction nut?"

"No."

"Well, there you go. Fans come in all shapes and sizes, and this particular one just doesn't want to be known."

"We'll see about that." Just then a car could be heard pulling up outside. Zoe's cell phone buzzed from her back pocket. "Shit." She jumped up with an apologetic glance. "That's my driver. I have to head to the studio. Let's talk about this later tonight!" She patted Mia's shoulder as she sped by.

"When will you be back?"

"Dunno!" she called back. "Take care of that knee!"

Once Zoe had scooted out the door and down the front steps, Mia was left alone with her thoughts. How strange things had been since she'd moved in. Back when she was packing up boxes and making future plans, all she'd hoped for was to immerse herself in the house of a great author and channel some of his magnificent literature-loving spirit. She had high expectations that involved harnessing some new form of positive energy and attacking her writing with gusto. As a fairly practical person, she didn't exactly expect ghosts or visions, but she had anticipated sensing more of the past, somehow. It never would have occurred to her when she signed her life away to stacks of escrow papers that life in the Bradbury house would bring mysterious notes and a homeless movie star. But she couldn't complain, could she? For, in fact, she had been writing and she had been inspired. By what or by whom wasn't entirely clear, but things were shifting. She could feel the change almost rising up from the floorboards, buzzing its way through her limbs. The only problem was it all felt so out of Mia's control.

FOURTEEN

⌒

*L*ater in the week, Zoe arrived home in the middle of the day, ringing the bell. It was unusually bright and sunny for a November afternoon, and Mia was met with the sun's full glare as she opened the door. Blinking like a mole emerging from hibernation, she peered outside. Having temporarily given up on her plan of daily walks due to her injury, she'd regretfully placed her search for the mystery man on hold. Instead, she harnessed all of her energy into work. She'd been writing at her desk for hours, hardly aware of the agreeable temperature outdoors. Since her fall, she'd ventured only as far as her room, the kitchen, and the study, hobbling a triangular path with a great deal of grumbling. Her knee, now a sickening hue of purple, still hurt terribly. She did not enjoy the experience of having to open the front door.

"Where's your key?" she asked, shading her eyes.

"In my pocket, but I can't reach it." Zoe stood before her in cropped shorts; a black shirt was rolled up at the elbows and tied into a knot around her middle, revealing her smooth, girlish stomach. Her petite arms were strained, wrapped around a substantial piece of furniture. It looked like a chaise longue. Standing back a bit was Zoe's driver, perspiring in the midday heat under his suit and tie and attempting to keep his balance on the stone steps while holding an identical chaise.

"Good grief, where are those going?" Mia asked, stepping aside.

Zoe and her driver, a straight-lipped older gentleman, entered the foyer, clumsily banging up against the sides of the hall as they maneuvered past Mia and in the direction of her bedroom.

"In the backyard!" Zoe called over her shoulder. "You and I are gonna sit in the sun and enjoy the day!"

Mia stood perplexed. She wasn't used to Zoe being so pushy. She also wasn't accustomed to random furniture deliveries at her door. Struggling to keep up with her bum knee, Mia followed the two of them into her bedroom. She found the French doors flung wide open and watched in dumb silence as Zoe and the man lugged the chairs onto the brick patio.

Limping past her unmade bed and heap of dirty clothes in the corner, Mia felt a little prickling of heat rise on the back of her neck. She was annoyed Zoe and some stranger had just traipsed through her messy refuge. As thoughtful as Zoe could be at times, Mia considered this private invasion a fairly thoughtless act. "Why did you bring those through my room?" she asked. "You could've just gone up the side of the house!"

If Zoe noticed that she'd agitated her grumpy housemate,

she didn't acknowledge it. "Dunno." She shrugged. "I guess I thought it would be easier going through the house, but now I see that the path over there would've been better." She thanked her driver, who wordlessly gave a curt nod and let himself out the same way he'd come. "He's very serious, isn't he?" Zoe giggled as he left.

Mia stood, hands on hips, waiting for an explanation.

"Girard, the film's director, says my character needs to be fit and tan. He says I'm too pale. They want me to get a spray tan, but I hate those things. You always leave stinking like burned skin and BO."

"So you'd rather sit out here and get skin cancer instead?" Mia surveyed the pair of obviously used patio chairs. Their tan leather straps were rough and distressed in the places where they stretched around lean bronze framing. They had a faded quality to them, like a pair of jeans that had been put through the wash one too many times. Still, their overall design was pleasant enough, and they'd undoubtedly fit in with the home's already worn-in look.

Hoping to sell Mia on the idea, Zoe sprawled out on one and contorted herself into an exaggerated model's pose. Even when she was being silly, this girl was a natural beauty. She jutted her hip to one side and pushed her lips into a pout, as if she were in a sexy lingerie ad. She ran a free hand along the straps. "They're vintage Brown Jordan. You like?"

"How do you know what vintage Brown Jordan furniture is?"

Zoe sat up. "Oh, my mom used to be all into antiques and home decor. She usually couldn't afford the nice things she bought, but that never really stopped her. We had a couple of chairs like this once." Her voice trailed off for a minute and she dropped her pose. There was something sad behind her eyes that betrayed her lightness. As if snapping herself out of a trance, she turned toward Mia and smiled. "Anyway, Girard gave the cast the afternoon off, so I had my driver help me find a patio store. These were out back. Aren't they cool?"

Mia surveyed the deserted yard. The flowerbeds were bone dry, the terra-cotta pots sat empty, and the garden area looked like a flower graveyard, with dead rosebush stumps protruding from the barren earth. The lawn was browning and in desperate need of a long drink. A few shrubs on the edge still clung to life, with only a smattering of green foliage left. Miraculously, an optimistic-looking fruit tree stood its ground in the corner, not willing to give in just yet. It stood like a pillar of hope in the otherwise forgotten landscape. The image of it all, with skeletons of florae that had long ago flourished with life, served as a reminder of what was probably once a lovely backyard.

Hadn't Mia planned to rejuvenate the rose garden? Wasn't the appeal of her bedroom mostly because it opened up to a bit of greenery? She was sure Mrs. Bradbury had devoted hours tending to her flowers in this very spot. It would be a dishonor not to keep the garden going. Mia suddenly felt ashamed for neglecting this special section of the home. The backyard deserved to be brought to life again. Now, thanks to Zoe, Mia was reminded of this.

She exhaled, letting the anger go out of her. "Yes, they're cool indeed," she said. "I can't remember the last time I lay in the sun. I have to put my leg up anyway; might as well be out here." Mia nodded at her still inflated knee.

"Well, what are we waiting for?" Zoe jumped up and trotted off in the direction of her room. "I'll meet you back here in five!"

It was there on the redbrick patio of the timeworn house that the two of them whiled away the day. The blissful sun angled its rays into the yard, warming their bodies and coloring their cheeks. Zoe lay uninhibited, exposing nearly every inch of her creamy complexion in a barely there string bikini. Mia accompanied her, self-consciously sweating in a much more modest cotton tank top and shorts. There was nothing as humbling as resting next to a beautiful actress half her age in nothing but beach attire. Tugging at the hem of last season's shorts, Mia was keenly aware of her dimpled thighs and flappy arms.

There was a time when she used to be in moderately good shape, taking full advantage of Carson's built-in home gym. But that was a few years back, before the failed book deal and shattered relationship, and before depression had set in, causing a lack of interest in pretty much everything, including her appearance. Reflecting on all of this, Mia silently chastised herself as she lay next to Zoe. She should start taking better care of herself. Maybe she'd go out and buy one of those juicers and throw herself into a nutrition regimen. Anything would help at this point.

Not caring to dwell on her health any longer, Mia scanned the yard. "I can't believe I've never spent any time out here before today." The patio was perched on the hillside, giving a view of the street below. It offered an entirely new perspective of the neighborhood and its renovated bungalows. Content, she stretched her limbs like a languid cat and wiggled her pale toes. Giving in to the luxury of it all, she let the sun's warmth cover her like a blanket.

Zoe had been texting on her phone, letting out little chuckles and guffaws as responses pinged back at her. Her fingers moved with warp speed, her thumbs punching and clicking secret messages and inside jokes to someone on the other end. Mia wondered who it was that captivated Zoe's attention. Perhaps it was a boy? After a while, Zoe set aside the phone and pushed a pair of metallic aviators up the bridge of her nose. Angling her chin toward the sun, she remarked, "It's kinda great, right? The only thing that would make it better would be a couple of blended margaritas. Big, slushy ones with salt around the rim!" Whether she'd meant to say this aloud or not, it was too late. Like a gluttonous child who required something sweet, her greedy desire had betrayed her.

Mia stiffened. Zoe wanted alcohol. Was this typical? Did everyone in recovery talk openly about missing his or her vices? Probably, Mia guessed. But then again, if Zoe was fantasizing over a cocktail, it might be a red flag about her sobriety. Maybe abstaining for a few months was her limit. Perhaps she was tired of being the good girl. Mia's pulse quickened; she felt the weight of responsibility pressing down on her. Her relaxation succumbed to fluttering anxiety. Now what?

"So . . . um . . . is that what you used to drink a lot of?" she ventured cautiously. "Margaritas?"

"Not really," Zoe flipped on her side to face Mia. "Don't worry; I'm not gonna run and make a drink or anything. I'm not stupid."

"Oh, good," Mia strained to relax. "I mean, good for you."

"Besides, you don't have any alcohol here anyway." Her comment hung in the air like a toxic cloud. Mia had absolutely no idea if Zoe was being sarcastic or if she'd been scouring the cupboards for forbidden beverages. At Emma's urging, Mia had gotten rid of the few wine bottles she kept in the house. She hadn't wanted there to be any temptation for her new guest, but even more selfishly, she hadn't wanted to deal with someone potentially losing control in her house.

"Very funny." Mia opted to act as if she got Zoe's joke. She was completely out of her element.

"I can say things like that to you," Zoe said. "If I said that around my sponsor, he'd probably threaten to lock me up again."

"You were locked up?"

"No, not really. Rehab was voluntary." She hooked her fingers in the air, making quote marks. "It just felt like a prison sometimes. A metaphorical prison, you know?"

"Oh, right," Mia said. She didn't know if it was right or not. All she knew at that moment was that she was very uneasy. "But are you glad you went?"

"Yeah, I needed to go and get my head straight. I was just really stressed out and I partied way too much. But rehab was hard because I was living with a bunch of strangers and forced to follow rules and a schedule that I wasn't used to. I felt like all my choices were taken away." A shadow of vulnerability crossed Zoe's face, reminiscent of the apprehensive and weary girl that walked through the door on that first day. Seeing this side of Zoe made Mia's heart drop. She much preferred to see the optimistic girl who had a lighthearted smile with the crooked tooth. But this girl's life wasn't as simple as that. Of course it wasn't, Mia corrected herself. Zoe had demons that she was going to be fighting for a long time, and it was naive to think the mere act of taking her in and offering her tea and idle conversation would remedy all of that. But for now, Zoe had opened up to her, and that had to be a good sign.

FIFTEEN

⌒

For the remainder of the week, Mia focused most of her energy on writing. As the words poured out, she kneaded them like doughy clay, molding and shaping them together to form a story. Pages were slowly forming into what she hoped would be a manuscript. Mia knew that what she had was something worth holding on to, and because of this, she carefully guarded her work. If she gave it enough time and attention, she might have something real by the end.

During this time she saw little of Zoe, who had been working all hours of the day and well into the night. Mia tried to keep a watchful eye, but worry continued to fester away inside her as she witnessed Zoe drag herself through the door at late hours, often irritable and always drained. The weary actress would come in the door carting a thick script and jumbo-sized coffee drinks. Her once glowing complexion seemed sallow and pallid, her clothes were disheveled, and her nails appeared chewed down to the nub.

Mia did her best not to probe, but she gathered from the

few comments Zoe made that things with the demanding Girard weren't going well. Whatever enthusiasm Zoe may have had about starting this film was being whittled down into bitter obligation. According to Zoe, Girard had made it known to the cast and crew that he was over budget and behind schedule. Zoe and the other actors seemed to be taking the brunt of his wrath as he feverishly attempted to squeeze every inch of life out of the actors as well as the production schedule. All Mia could do was lend an ear and usher a zombielike Zoe off to bed.

"It's not good," she said to Carson one morning over the phone. "She's got bags under her eyes the size of Texas."

"Uh-huh." Carson didn't share her concern. "That happens when movies are in full production mode. People lose sleep. I'm sure it's not the first time, Mia."

Mia shook the phone with a fist and considered tossing it across her bedroom before returning it to her ear. "I'm not an idiot, Carson. I realize actors work strange hours. But what if all this stress puts her right back where she started? What if she relapses?"

Carson thought for a moment. "I don't know. Maybe she will, maybe she won't. But if the girl can't act, then her career is flat over." He softened a bit. "Mia, I appreciate you worrying about her. You have a good heart and Zoe's lucky to have you in her corner. But don't sound the alarm bells quite yet. Give her a chance to rise to the occasion, okay?"

Why was it every time she talked to Carson lately he was always insinuating she needed to calm down? Was she over-reacting? She didn't consider herself a hysterical person. But between her growing worry over Zoe and the neighborhood mystery man nagging at her thoughts, she felt she was turning into a crazy person. She'd never been in this position.

Sensing her angst, Carson interjected. "How about we talk about something nicer?"

"Like what?"

"Like, how about going to dinner with me tomorrow night?" His voice rose at the end, betraying his confidence.

Mia picked at a hangnail and thought for a moment. Where was he going with this? "Dinner?"

"Yes, dinner. As in me, you, and an exchange of pleasant conversation over a meal. Sound familiar?" He was mocking her now.

"Yeah, it sounds familiar." A dozen images of shared romantic dinners popped into Mia's mind. She shook her head, attempting to rattle the memories loose. "But why right now? Aren't things a little hectic at the moment?"

"Things are always hectic, and why not right now? Come on, it'll do you good to get out of that house and into the land of the living."

It was true, since her fall she'd spent far too much time indoors. Because of this, her world had become small, confined mostly to the indoors, to write and play watchdog to Zoe. She realized this was probably not the healthiest thing. Her knee was healing, its bruise fading into a noxious yellow, thus eliminating her excuse to hide at home with her feet up on the sofa. Perhaps an evening out with Carson would be a nice change of pace. Without overthinking it, she accepted his offer and agreed to join him the following night.

ARRIVING THE NEXT EVENING AT A WEST HOLLYWOOD eatery, Mia paid the Uber driver she'd used rather than worrying about navigating behind the wheel with her bum knee, and checked her makeup in her compact mirror one final time. Carson had selected a restaurant that had just recently opened. *New place, fresh start,* Mia thought. When they were dating, they used to frequent the best sushi restaurants in town, always making a game of choosing the most complicated hand rolls on the menu and ordering things like dragon rolls and spicy tuna with eel. They'd spend hours sipping hot sake and making eyes at one another. But that was then. Tonight, Mia wondered if Carson had been careful not to suggest one of their old haunts for fear of dredging up the past.

She met him outside a small French bistro, Chez Pierre, glad she'd insisted upon arriving separately to avoid it looking too much like a date. She'd convinced herself that they were friends now and that this dinner was to be about friendly conversation and a night off from her worries. Between stewing over the identity and motivations of her mystery man and hovering over Zoe, she welcomed this night out, however cautious she might be about her ex's intentions.

Carson, on the other hand, was brimming with enthusiasm as she approached him. He'd been waiting in front of the contemporary new hot spot, unaffected by the steady stream of patrons flowing through an already crowded entrance. Beautiful women strutted past him in posh cocktail dresses and revealing halter tops. They reminded Mia of a pack of sleek and dangerous jaguars out on the prowl. Many of them shot ravenous glances at Carson as they passed. Carson, who was out of his usual jeans for once and dressed in a sharp sport coat and slacks, remained locked on Mia. His unflinching stare made her heart skip a beat in a moment of weakness. *Be strong*, she told herself. *You're here to be his friend, not his lover.* She repeated this a few more times in her head before she allowed him to reach out and kiss her cheek.

"You look lovely," he said, placing a palm on the small of her back and guiding her through the maze of patrons. He ignored everyone else save for her.

"Thank you." She accepted the compliment. It was true; she had taken the time to pick out a sheer, pale blue dress from her closet, buoyant from the prospect of a night on the town. After a long, steamy shower in which she'd shaved her much-neglected legs, she'd perched in front of the mirrored vanity, straightening the unruly waves in her hair and dabbing pink rouge on her cheeks. She'd taken care with her mascara, and even attempted to tame her wildly dark eyebrows, using a disturbingly sharp pair of tweezers that Emma had once recommended. When she was finished primping, Mia had lingered in front of the vanity and pondered over how Mrs. Bradbury might have done the same in that very spot. Did Bradbury's wife also feel excitement before going out with her husband? Mia knew that she must have been deeply devoted to Bradbury, considering they were wed for over fifty years. Mia wondered if she'd ever have a relationship that long-lasting. The notion was difficult to conceive.

As much as Mia didn't want her date with Carson to be a romantic one, she had to admit that she enjoyed the idea of being paid attention to. It had been a long time since she'd gone out with a man, let alone participated in anything even remotely amorous. So even if it was just Carson and it was not officially a date, she decided to let go of her trepidation in the spirit of having a nice time.

"You know, I didn't think you'd take me up on my invitation," Carson said as they sat down and perused the wine list. "You're usually so against spending time with me."

She thought for a moment. "Carson, let's not talk about what usually happens with us. No good can come of that. How about we just keep it simple tonight?" She was surprised at how easily she could let it all go for now. It wasn't really all that simple to ignore the past and act as if they were free of complications. But it was exactly what she needed for just one night: to loosen herself from all the worry and suspicion that had tangled itself around her like a web. Tonight she wanted to be free.

Carson seemed more than willing to agree on this point. In a celebratory tone, he ordered an expensive bottle of Malbec and clinked glasses with Mia. She noticed him fidget a bit while they perused the menu. He repeatedly brought his hand to his neck, straightening his collar and swiveling his head like he was trying to free himself of a noose. Mia wondered if she'd always possessed the ability to make him this uncomfortable. Had all the distance between them made him uneasy about being together? She studied him now, as he fiddled with the place setting and glanced around the room. Was it possible that Carson had changed? Was he capable of growth? He caught her staring and raised his glass again in a silent toast.

After a short time the drinks took their effect, easing them both into a warm and fuzzy state. Conversation came effortlessly as they carried on into the evening over long courses of delicate French dishes that melted on Mia's tongue: steamed mussels and creamy scallops, tender medallions, and duck confit. The more she ate, the more she licked her fingers and lost herself in the pure indulgence of the delicious food. Endorphins buzzed through her like bees over honey. Swirling her wine into little whirlpools, she relaxed into her seat and let the burgundy liquid mesmerize her into a dreamy trance. Her eyelids turned drowsy with satisfaction. The alcohol was going to her head. Ever since Zoe had moved in, Mia hadn't had much to drink. Her tolerance was now remarkably low. "That was wonderful," she said with a lazy smile. "That may have been the best meal I've had in forever."

"I'm so glad you liked it." Caron's stare was deep and inviting. He leaned across the table and placed a steady hand over hers, letting the heat build between them. "I miss times like these with you." His comment was sweet and subtle, but loaded with meaning. He was her friend, yes, but he was always willing to ask for more. Their hands lingered on the table like two magnets, the energy of their touch generating an unavoidable pull.

It would have been easy to slip into familiar habits, for Mia to be enveloped in Carson's intoxicating embrace. It would take nothing at all to accept his advance and get lost in pleasure. Part of her was rising with need. There were places of her body that hadn't been touched, hadn't felt the intensity of another person for so long. She could almost feel herself curling into him, ready to give herself over to desire. She said nothing as he paid the bill and led her out of the restaurant, his strong arm hooked around the curve of her waist. She didn't protest when he summoned the valet and escorted her to the front seat of his Mercedes. Sliding in, Mia inhaled the lustrous leather interior that smelled entirely of Carson. It sent a tingle of desire through her body, its effect like a potent drug.

"Where to?" he asked as he climbed into the driver's seat. Mia watched his hand grip the gearshift, wondering if it might come to rest on her thigh.

"My place," she purred. She felt sleepy and dreamy, secured in the cocoon of his car.

"As you wish." Carson sped off into the night, both of them intensely aware of what awaited them.

As they rounded the corner into her neighborhood, something caught Mia's attention. Inching forward in her seat, she rubbed the haze from her eyes and tried to piece together what she was seeing. It was like being awakened from a dream and asked to solve a puzzle. Pressing her face near the dashboard, she registered a row of cars obstructing her quiet street. As Carson eased up the road, they came upon several cars parked in a haphazard arrangement in her driveway. It was as if their owners had all arrived in a hurry.

"What the hell is going on here?" She unfastened her seat belt and reached for the door.

"Whoa," Carson said. "Wait for me to pull over." He pointed the nose of his car at an angle and double-parked behind a polished cobalt Mustang. "This doesn't look good."

"You think?" Mia snapped wide awake, her blood already boiling. Not waiting for Carson to cut the engine, she swung her feet out of the car and charged up the front steps. Whatever romantic illusions she'd had earlier evaporated and were now replaced with surging rage. She shoved open the front door and scanned the scene.

The first thing she noticed was all of the people inside her house. A dozen kids Zoe's age were piled on and around her living room sofa. They were all limbs and laughter, sprawled out as if they belonged there. Several of them were sipping from what looked like Mia's collection of juice glasses. On the floor, an empty bottle of wine lay askew next to a girl with an alarmingly short skirt. The girl's shoes were off; her thin, long legs stretched out like a young gazelle's. She gazed out from under a fringe of thick false eyelashes and caught Mia's glare. Unaffected, she offered a zoned-out smile and went back to texting on her phone.

Mia's nostrils flared as swiveled around in search of Zoe. Guitar strumming came from the direction of the kitchen, where more laughter and loud voices echoed off the walls. With frantic strides, Mia toured the disheveled dining room. She pushed past a cluster of people, who milled around with beer cans in their hands. As she noticed more empty wine bottles and open packs of cigarettes scattered across the table, Mia's heart sank at the sight of watery rings and bottle caps covering the furniture. A couple of her wooden chairs were flung down on the floor, indicating some kind of abrupt exit or even a scuffle. More partiers were gathered outside the patio door, and a trail of smoke wound up through the air and filtered through the open windows. A boy outside called out to someone farther down the street, and a set of girls cackled like garish hyenas. Mia cringed; she was sure their loud voices were not what her neighbors wanted to hear.

Moving through the breakfast room and into the kitchen, Mia at last discovered Zoe. She was sitting on the kitchen counter, her bare legs spilling out from cropped shorts and dangling over the side with her fuzzy boots swinging back and forth. Zoe's eyes were closed as her head rested on the shoulder of a guy with too much gel in his hair and a guitar in his lap. The boy had ridiculously chiseled features and wore an arrogant smirk. Mia instantly pegged him to be Zoe's costar, Brody something-or-other, who was known as a teen heartthrob on the rise. More bodies blocked Mia's way as she tried to push farther into the room. They were carelessly leaning against appliances and cradling bottles of cheap beer. A few of them held Mia's glasses, which were filled with ominous dark liquid. The stench of stale cigarettes and alcohol hit her before she could open her mouth. As she looked around, Mia's heart dropped. Her beautiful house that she'd left only hours before had been turned into a frat party.

"Zoe!" The strength of Mia's voice shocked even herself. She stood erect in the center of the tiled floor, clenching her fists and boring holes into her housemate with her eyes. Mia felt as if her hair were standing on end as lightning bolts of fury tore through her.

Someone let out a gasp. A girl in a dress ran from the room. Zoe bolted off the counter and stumbled forward, her face pale with fear. "Oh, Mia. I can explain . . ."

"Don't bother," Mia fumed. "Tell your friends it's time to go." She wanted to yell and scream and ask Zoe what she could have possibly been thinking and how dare she have a full-blown party in her house. She shook right to her very core, her mind clouded over with rage, and she was unable to get her thoughts out fast enough. Turning on her heel, Mia stormed out, only to run smack into a panting Carson. "Get out of my way!" She shoved him, causing him to stumble sideways, and made for her bedroom. Her mystified date called after her, but she didn't stop. Hot, angry tears clouded her vision as she made her way to her bedroom and slammed the door. Throwing herself onto her bed, she cursed Carson, Zoe, her sister, and everyone else who had trampled all over her private sanctuary. This was her house, her dream, and they'd all gone and invaded it with their stupid, self-centered interests. She should have known better than to let them in—the whole lot of them.

SIXTEEN

⌒

*M*ia remained locked in her room for the rest of
the night, ignoring the commotion just beyond
her door. Carson must have gone home,
because Mia didn't hear his voice in the house after a few
minutes. What followed was a lot of grumbling and disappointed declarations as Zoe ushered her friends from the
house. The owner of the Mustang screeched from the driveway,
accelerating with a high pitch and sending a chill down Mia's
spine. Zoe might have tried to explain or even apologize, but
Mia had jammed in her earbuds, opting to listen to her iPod
at full blast. She stripped out of her dress and rubbed a
scalding washcloth over her face, wiping away all traces of
her makeup and the evening's loveliness along with it. With
a heavy heart, she flopped back onto her bed and shrunk into
a fetal position. Why must everyone always disappoint her
so? She lay that way for a long time, miserable and lonely and
mystified at her own misfortune.

Slumber washed over her in a weary fog that night. Her

puzzling dreams returned—the papery dragons scrambling about, their jagged talons scratching across the ground as they traveled. Miniature elfin creatures, whose alien antennae bobbed about, floated in and out of focus, taunting her with their impish ways. These curious images didn't necessarily constitute nightmares, but were more like murky clues to a mystery her mind could not unlock. She awoke only once, opening her eyes to scan the inky darkness around her. Listening, she heard nothing and fell back into a fitful sleep. She dreamed again. This time it rained hundreds of squares of white paper, folded and creased. They fell from an opaque, cloud-filled sky, crackling as they crashed down at her feet and piling up around her ankles. As the rains delivered more messages, she waded through a river of paper that rose higher as she went. Soon she was swimming through the river, pushing aside papery currents that threatened to carry her under. In her dream, she scooped up handfuls of notes and tried to open them, but they were sealed tight, like locks without a key. Giving up, she floated along, to where she did not know.

Unrested and irritable, Mia rose with the sun. At 6:00 a.m. she faced the bathroom mirror and surveyed her bloodshot eyes. The combination of wine and a terrible night's sleep had taken its toll on her appearance. Her usually narrow features were now dreadfully puffy, her hair was wild, and dusty bits of sleep were gathered on her lashes. A deep crease ran down the right side of her cheek. *What a mess you are*, she told her reflection. Without further scrutiny, she located her sneakers and shorts and pulled a baseball cap low over her forehead. Today she would not be seen. Avoiding the mess that likely awaited her in the rest of the house, she unlocked the patio doors and slipped away down the side of the garden.

The damp morning mist encircled her as she stepped onto the sidewalk and determined her route. Rubbing her palms together, she blew into them and hopped up and down to get the blood flowing. Now that the Santa Anas were gone, a crisp November chill hung in the air. Zipping her hoodie up around her bare neck, Mia decided to walk in the opposite direction from her last outing. Only partially on the lookout for her mystery man, Mia set her legs in motion. At the moment, she was more interested in getting out of the house and into some fresh air than in playing detective. This time, she would pay special attention to the topography. She moved up the street, carefully picking her steps in the dark, on the thin stretch of sidewalk between front lawns and the roots of aging elms. She liked how this section of her community was the home to wizened-looking deciduous trees. They gave a little nod to the changing seasons with the shedding of their leaves. Southern California certainly wasn't known for its fall foliage, but in older neighborhoods like Cheviot Hills, a pleasing assortment of mature trees filled in the otherwise palm-dominated scenery.

The sky was transforming into a watercolor blue as the sun crept over the horizon, pushing light over the hills. A couple of cars passed as people made their way to work, their engines momentarily drowning out the morning calls of the birds. Other than these brief interruptions, Mia was alone. The solitude put her in a reflective mood as her steps fell into a steady rhythm. Moving up the next block, she replayed the previous night's events in her head.

For starters, she'd almost slept with Carson. This realization hit her like a plunging blow. With all the chaos of the night, she'd completely disregarded the details of her date. *My god*, she thought, *that would have altered everything.* Is that what she even wanted? She didn't think so, but she couldn't really be sure. Carson had been so attentive and caring over dinner. He'd looked into her eyes and ignored all of the much more beautiful women who had drifted in and out of the restaurant. He'd held her hand and listened when she talked. Most of all, her ex-lover had triggered in her a certain amount of genuine lust, warm and tingly and difficult to dismiss. He'd been so sexy. Good grief, what was she thinking? And what was *he* thinking? He knew better than anyone that he was not a one-woman kind of guy and that this very issue had been the root cause of all of their trouble. Hadn't it?

When they'd been living together, he had apologized profusely after TMZ aired a video of him canoodling with a well-stacked brunette at an LA club, promised to do better when photos of his Catalina getaway with a fame-seeking blonde splashed across *Us Weekly*, and begged Mia to stay when she packed up her bags after a rather drunken twenty-year-old appeared outside their gate asking to be let in to see her boyfriend. It had been all too much for Mia to handle.

Since then, as time progressed, Mia was forced to consider the possibility that her own actions might have played a part in the relationship's demise. It was quite likely that despite all of his antics and self-absorbed skirt chasing, she alone was responsible for her isolation. Looking back, she'd held Carson at bay, choosing to wallow in the self-pity of her failures all on her own. After her book flopped, she'd spent a considerable amount of time erecting a glass house in which to live, only allowing Carson to view her from the other side, but never to enter.

On the other hand, Carson would be turning fifty soon. Maybe his age was catching up to him. Maybe he was tired of the game and wanted to work his way toward settling down. Perhaps it wasn't any of those things. Like a wolf on the hunt, he might have sensed Mia's weaknesses, recognized her vulnerability, and planned to pounce in his moment of opportunity. Or perhaps it wasn't even as calculated as all of that. In the end, she had to face the notion that maybe she and Carson were destined to be together. But the time to address such an idea was not today.

Stepping into the foyer, Mia held her breath and prepared for the worst. She expected broken bottles and scuffmarks on her wood floors. She predicted coming home to a slapdash cleaning job and an inconsiderate atmosphere. Slipping off her shoes, she walked over to her sofa and inspected the spot where, hours earlier, strangers had taken over. But the couch was empty, the pillows were fluffed, and her cashmere throw was folded neatly over the side. Even the floor looked newly wiped down, the wood grain shining more than usual. It appeared as if someone had taken a mop to the entire room. Intrigued, Mia moved through the dining room and discovered the same polished effect that she'd found in the first room. The windows were ajar, allowing for a fresh breeze to float into the house. The water rings had been rubbed from the table and the chairs were righted to their correct position. This was not at all what Mia thought she'd find. Curious, she entered the kitchen and was met with yet another clean room. The counters were spotless, the trash was empty, and the floors showed not a mark. Was this Carson or Zoe? She stopped and listened for any signs of life, but the house remained still.

Mystified, Mia made her way into her bedroom and came to a stop at the edge of her bed. A glass pitcher rested on her nightstand, a cascade of yellow and white daisies spilling over the sides. Next to the arrangement stood a plain folded card with the words *I'm sorry* written in curvy feminine letters.

SEVENTEEN

⌒

The morning after Mia discovered the flowers, both women stood in the hazy morning light of the front hall and stared at one another. At sunrise, Mia had been heading out for her daily walk. At precisely the same time, Zoe came along, dragging her usual suspicious bag with her, on her way to an early call time. The timing did not please Mia. Zoe faced her, remorseful and weary, and fixed a pair of worried eyes on her as she launched into an apology. Running into her at such an early hour took Mia off guard. She'd wanted nothing more than to greet the day in solitude and head out into the quiet of the dawn's soft light. Now she had no choice but to be held captive while Zoe rambled on about her excuse for having thrown a party. Busying herself with tightening her shoelaces and zipping up her fleece sweatshirt, Mia halfheartedly listened to the explanations laid out before her.

"It wasn't planned or anything like that," Zoe said. "My friends were supposed to come get me so we could go out, go to some club. But Brody got here first and said we should wait for the others. Then a few random people showed up with these girls I know and then we were still waiting and someone opened a few beers, and before I knew it everyone was hanging out." The words spilled out in a long trail of excuses. "We were gonna leave, but I guess we lost track of time and more people kept showing up wanting to hang out. It just sort of happened."

Mia finished with her laces and stood. Tilting her head, she raised an eyebrow. "So how did all those people know how to get here in the first place?"

Zoe's eyes widened. "Brody, I guess. I sure didn't tell them. Only a couple of friends from work even know where I live these days."

"Brody, huh?" Mia crossed her arms. "Are you guys an item?" She may have sounded like an old biddy, but she didn't care. Zoe had put her in this position and now she was left to play the part of the disapproving guardian. Mia didn't like that Brody kid anyway. Just by the look of his snarky smile and ridiculous hairdo, she could tell he was bad news. And what kind of a friend drinks alcohol around someone who's supposed to be sober? Mia couldn't remember if she'd seen Brody holding any kind of drink that night, but somehow she felt he was not the best influence on Zoe.

Mia didn't wait for an answer. She could already tell that this costar of Zoe's had designs on her. "Zoe, your so-called friends were all drinking and they were in your house. Well, my house, actually, but they knew you lived here. Don't they all know you've been in rehab?"

Zoe rolled her eyes to the ceiling and back. "Yeah, they know. But I wasn't drinking, I swear." Her twenty-three-year-old tone was growing more defensive. "It doesn't bother me."

Mia let out a huff. "Sorry, but I don't buy that. Maybe you weren't drinking, but everyone else was. What kind of friend stands around you all night with cocktails in their hand?" It was maddening to believe that Zoe could be so daft. Didn't she see those people for what they were, hangers-on, moochers, who wanted nothing more than an invitation to party with a hot celebrity? The entire conversation was enraging her all over again. The soft spot that had opened up after Mia discovered the clean house and daisy bouquet was beginning to harden and close. She wasn't totally out of touch—she realized kids needed to have fun—but this was too much to handle. People make mistakes; hell, she made mistakes all the time. And because Zoe had cleaned up her mess and owned up to it, Mia had momentarily relaxed. But this conversation confirmed that she couldn't fully trust Zoe now.

She might be able to forgive her for her error in judgment, but the bigger questioned loomed: How many more mistakes were on their way? Her gut did a somersault. Hadn't she taken her role as Zoe's guardian seriously enough? She'd made a promise to Carson to look out for Zoe, but how good of a job had she really done with this? Maybe she'd been more concerned about being Zoe's friend than anything else. Had she failed at this, too?

Zoe tightened her grip on the bag's handle. "You don't understand. I'm fine. It's okay if someone has a beer around me. I'm not going to tell my friends not to drink. That's their decision, not mine." She was putting her acting skills to use, Mia could tell. She'd made too much of an effort to emphasize sounding casual about the whole affair. She didn't look casual, though. She looked stressed, and the dark semicircles under her eyes were still hanging on. She was haggard, and Mia could see it as plainly as the nose on her face.

"Zoe, you may think you're fine. And maybe you are. But I don't think it's wise to surround yourself with reminders of your old bad habits. It's not healthy."

Zoe jerked her tote over her shoulder, her eyes ablaze. "What do you know about my sobriety?" The apologetic girl had suddenly vanished and left an incensed one in her place. "You don't know anything about me! I'm sorry my friends and I used your house, but you have no right to judge them. Just because I sleep in one of your rooms doesn't mean you get to know everything about me. Nobody does!" With that, Zoe stormed out the door. On the last stair, her foot caught on the stone walkway, causing her to trip and stumble forward. Mia moved to help her, but was headed off by Zoe's driver. He pulled to the curb and got out quickly to assist Zoe with her things before he ushered her into the car. By the time Mia reached the street, they were driving away, leaving her bewildered and alone.

"SO YOU'RE TELLING ME SHE HAD A PARTY IN YOUR house and you let her get away with it?" Emma inquired on the phone later that day.

"I didn't let her have a party," Mia said. "I wasn't home. By the time Carson and I returned, things were in full swing. When I got here I let her know I was pissed off and then she shooed everybody out."

"Uh-huh. You and Carson came back together?" Emma let the words sit in her mouth like something hard to swallow. "What were you doing out with him in the first place?" *Here it comes,* Mia thought. The old "Carson is bad for you" speech that she'd heard a million times before. But this time it wasn't Carson's fault.

"He had nothing to do with it," Mia said. Lying on her back in her bedroom, she counted cracks in the ceiling and waited for the inevitable.

"You bet he had something to do with it!" Emma said. "If it wasn't for him and his stupid demand that you take in this mess of a girl, none of this would have happened."

Mia might as well have been eleven years old all over again, receiving a lecture from her older sister on how she needed to grow up and stop leaving her dirty clothes all over their shared bathroom. To be fair, Emma had slipped on one of Mia's discarded socks and nearly split her forehead open on the bathroom counter, but being on the opposite end of Emma's lectures was not acceptable anymore. Mia knew she'd made mistakes, but why did Emma always have to act so perfect?

She breathed hard into receiver. "Just give it up, will you?"

"Excuse me?"

Mia continued, "You may be right. I may be the big fat

idiot who's letting the world take her for a ride. But could you just shut up and let me figure it out for once?" This was the second time she'd insinuated her sister could shove her criticism where the sun didn't shine, and it felt pretty good.

"Fine."

"Fine."

Awkward silence filled the void between them. "Well, the kids have been asking about you." Emma did her best to change the subject. "I told them maybe you would come for Thanksgiving again this year. Is that something I'm allowed to say without you telling me to shut up?"

Mia chuckled. "Oh my god, Emma. You really are dramatic sometimes. I miss Michael and Anna, too. Thanksgiving is not for a couple of weeks, right? Let's talk closer to the date. I might need to wait and see what Zoe has planned. Something tells me I may need to keep an eye on her for the holidays."

"Well, I already told the kids that I thought you were coming. So think about it. And"—she paused—"if you have to, bring your charity case along with you—as long as she stays away from my wine!"

"Oh boy," Mia said.

"Oh boy is right. Good luck, sister."

EIGHTEEN

⌇

Out all day running errands, Mia returned home with sacks of groceries piled high in the backseat of her car. She'd spent an hour at Whole Foods, roaming the aisles, filling her cart with organic produce and protein powders, knowing she'd be making her health food–loving parents proud. She figured there was no time like the present to dig out her never-used blender and incorporate some fortifying nutrition into her diet. Too many things felt out of control for her recently. Developing a smoothie routine wasn't a big plan, but it felt like something she could manage, and with positive results. Right now, Mia needed something she could control.

Clearly her involvement in Zoe's life wasn't exactly going well. Mia wasn't sure what she'd expected the day she'd waited by the window for a strange girl to arrive. If she were like Emma, she would have had a well-designed plan and a contingent plan behind that one. When Emma was pregnant with her first child, Michael, she'd rubbed her growing belly and pored over an old-fashioned-looking book called *What to Expect When You're Expecting.* Mia watched her sister write out detailed feeding schedules, delicately fold tiny footed pajamas, and organize stacks of pint-sized diapers in anticipation of her new arrival. Emma made sure she'd done her homework, and was prepared with paraphernalia and research and knowledge. Mia marveled at her dedication on becoming a new mother. She'd admired Emma for the manner in which she was openly and completely committed to taking on her role. Her sister could be brave that way.

But in Mia's case, there was no way to really prepare for her new arrival of a strange young girl. There had been no book on how to properly care for a twenty-three-year-old actress in recovery. The only research available was from reading sensationalized tabloid stories that might or might not have been factual. No one had warned Mia of the possible mood swings and reckless behavior. There was no guide for what to do in case of emergency. More than that, Mia was not prepared for her heart to open up to this new person with the inquisitive soul and mesmerizing spirit. She had no way of knowing she'd develop a strong urge to protect Zoe and a desire to reprimand her at the same time. There had been no manual on how to speak to an otherwise motherless girl who was just becoming a woman herself, fully capable yet unable to avoid the land mines of love and temptation in her own life. Mia was at a loss.

Deciding she needed objective advice, she lugged her shopping bags inside and fished out her cell phone to dial her mother.

"Hello?" An airy voice as light as a feather answered on the other end. A distant whirring of what sounded like a washing machine hummed in the background. For an instant, the trace of warm dryer sheets and lavender hand cream filled Mia's senses. Envisioning her mother standing on the other end, her white-blonde hair fixed in a low bun, her sun-spotted hand wrapped around the phone, sent a pang of nostalgia tugging at Mia's heart. She was never particularly close to her mother, but she missed her nonetheless.

"Mom? It's me, Mia." Mia always felt the need to remind her mother which daughter was calling. Speaking on the phone wasn't something they typically did.

"Oh, hi, dear. Is everything okay?" Trudy Gladwell wasn't much of a phone talker. She'd always left the family commun-ication up to her husband, typically interjecting questions from somewhere in the background whenever the girl's father would ring them up. Because of this, her mother only made phone calls for emergencies and dinner reservations.

"Yes, Mom. Everything is fine. I just wanted to ask you something."

"Oh, that's fine, dear. Should I get your father? He's out front somewhere talking to that nosy neighbor of ours."

Mia could just imagine her father, hands tucked in his trouser pockets, rocking back onto his heels and patiently lending an ear to those more garrulous. "No, I don't need Dad. So Mom, was I terrible to you when I was a teenager?"

Her mother chortled, her breathy tone a faint breeze. "If you're asking me if living under the roof with two adolescent girls was easy, the answer is no. You were good girls, but that's not to say you didn't have your arguments and moments of hormonal ups and downs. But that's all part of life. Why are you asking?"

"Just wondering, that's all." Mia wasn't sure how much she should share about her current predicament. Her mother wasn't normally one to jump in and solve problems for her capable daughters.

"Is this about that young lady living in your extra bedroom? The one from the movies?"

"Yeah. I'm guessing Emma has filled you in?" Mia closed her eyes and pictured Emma chewing her mother's ear off with all kinds of tattletale gossip. She was sure her sister relished in being the messenger; she always had.

"As a matter of fact, she did. She seems to think this houseguest of yours is not entirely stable and it might be having an effect on you. Is this girl giving you trouble?"

This was the longest conversation Mia had had with her mother in—she couldn't remember when. Since her parents had moved to the opposite coast, the opportunities to catch up with their daily lives had been sparse. Maybe relocation had turned her mother into a phone person after all. "I don't know. I'm just not sure I'm cut out for this . . . this caring for someone who doesn't always want to be cared for."

The laughter returned. "Why, that's motherhood, Mia. Mothers of teenage daughters are doing this every day—nurturing their children until they are grown-up enough to make healthy decisions for themselves."

"But I'm not a mother. Zoe already has one of those, in France." Saying it out loud underscored just how strange it was.

"I think you just answered your own question. The woman is in France. You may not be this girl's mother, Mia, but it sounds like you're filling that role whether you planned it that way or not. The better question to ask is: Do you want to be that person?"

Mia ruminated on this for a long time after hanging up with her mother. Did she want to be that person for Zoe? It was a loaded question. If she was honest, she'd never wanted Zoe to arrive in the first place, but once she had, things turned out much differently from what she'd anticipated. Mia stared over her bags of thawing groceries and wondered where she went from there.

Going about her day, Mia tidied the house and did her best to ignore the barrage of dings on her cell phone, announcing Carson's texts. She wasn't ready to deal with him yet. Whatever he had to say could wait.

Guilt crept in anyway; Mia was conscious of the way she'd treated Carson at the end of their night together. She'd been loopy and lust-driven and not at all thinking clearly when she invited him to her house. That was a poor decision, for nothing good would come of hooking up with the man who'd already shattered her heart into a thousand tiny pieces. Regardless, it was shameful to have shoved and hollered at him the way she had. Unfortunately, this was how the pattern had always been with Carson; things would start out lovely but inevitably turn messy and complicated. It was like being drawn to the beautiful soft petals of a rose, only to reach out and be stuck by a piercing thorn. Carson didn't set out to be harmful; that was just the way things often went.

Mia needed a break from him. It was time to focus on her work and block out the rest of the noise in her head.

Leaving her phone to rest in the depths of a closed drawer, she headed upstairs to the seclusion of her office. As she came upon the stillness of Zoe's room, it was obvious that she was alone in the house. At the guest room door, Mia placed her palm on the exterior and contemplated entering. A handful of days had gone by, and she'd seen neither hide nor hair of Zoe. Their last encounter had been a chilly one at best. She guessed at the fact that Zoe was most likely avoiding her, not wanting to be scrutinized any further. Mia thought the distance would be a nice reprieve, but her mind was overrun with worry instead. Where had Zoe been spending her time after filming each day? Was she coupled up with Brody, hanging out at nightclubs and being led right into the mouth of temptation? Was she getting enough sleep? Was Girard pushing her too hard? All of these fears swirled ominously over Mia's head like gathering storm clouds.

Calling upon all of her willpower not to snoop in Zoe's room, she slipped farther down the hall. As she settled in at her desk, the computer monitor illuminated and blinked at her. For a long while, Mia just stared back, unable to move. She had to face reality; things were shifting. The plentiful well of inspiration from which she'd been greedily pulling recently was no longer full. She'd been through this before and could recognize the signs anywhere. Her writing, the surge of creativity that she'd had for weeks now, was slowly ebbing, like a tide moving away from the shore. Too many obstacles were in its way; the worry, the distractions, the hurt feelings all served as blockades in her brain. Unwilling to give in to the old familiar dread of writer's block, she forced her fingers onto the keyboard and began pounding away as if her life depended upon it.

⌣

NINETEEN

Mia never realized the act of whipping one's vitamins into a green froth could be so satisfying. After cramming her blender with handfuls of broad, leafy kale, chunks of apples and oranges, and a sprinkling of flax seed, she pressed a button and waited through the deafening noise while her sturdy little kitchen appliance produced a drinkable concoction. Prying the lid off the glass container, Mia felt as if she'd just performed a magic trick. And perhaps she had, because another whir of the thunderous machine produced a sleepy-eyed Zoe, standing beside her barefoot and tangle-haired.

"Well, good morning," Mia said. She pressed the off switch and gave a sheepish smile. "Sorry this is so loud. I didn't mean to wake you."

Zoe stumbled across the blue tile floor and leaned on the cabinet next to Mia. She squinched up her face and regarded the blender with a suspicious eye. Placing a hand over her throat, she eased closer to get a sniff of Mia's drink. "What exactly is in there?"

"Some veggies and a little fruit. I'm trying to be healthier." Mia twisted the pitcher free from its base and poured half of its contents into a cup. "Want to try some?"

"Ugh. No thanks." Zoe moved away and watched Mia gulp down the first third of her drink before speaking again. "I am hungry, though. Do we have anything good for breakfast?" She nodded at the refrigerator like a little kid eager for a snack.

Mia, who had been up for hours, energized from her morning walk and glad to have some interaction with Zoe, jumped at the chance to make breakfast. She had decided that the next chance she got alone with Zoe she'd make a genuine effort to get along. "I actually do have some turkey bacon and probably some toast. Does that sound good?"

Zoe's eyes brightened. "Yes, that sounds awesome. We didn't eat dinner last night and I was so burnt out when I came home that I just crashed." She rubbed at her mascara-smudged lashes.

"We?" Mia tried to sound nonchalant as she plucked ingredients from the refrigerator. She piled bread, butter, and a jar of blackberry jam on the counter while she waited for Zoe to respond.

"Girard had us shooting a scene until late. He's a maniac —he kept screaming and shaking his fists during people's lines. I think we ran one scene for like, two hours, just over and over. He's losing his mind." Zoe scratched her head like she was trying to dislodge the memory. Seeing her standing there in her oversized black T-shirt and newly tanned legs warmed Mia's heart a little. Whatever icy attitude Zoe had given her earlier in the week had now thawed to a civilized temperature. This is what Mia wanted, time to check in with Zoe and gauge whether or not she should remain worried. But as of that moment it just felt like a regular day; like two people making breakfast and discussing their schedule. Mia began frying the bacon while Zoe peppered her with details of life on the movie set.

She told Mia about the other actors and of the crew, whom she admitted were the real workers and were carrying pretty much the entire movie. At the mention of Brody, she made a face and said he was overly dramatic and selfish around the set. Mia didn't press her for details, but from the disgusted manner in which Zoe said his name, she gathered that the charm of the teen heartthrob had worn dull. Mia let out a breath of relief as she popped the bread into the toaster and encouraged Zoe to continue with her download.

"It got so bad last night that Carson had to come down to the set and manage Girard's ridiculous temper." Zoe climbed into what was becoming her usual position in the kitchen, perched near the sink with her smooth legs dangling over the counter. As she spoke she fiddled with an orange, only half committing to peeling it.

"Carson was there?" Mia hoped her voice hadn't betrayed her.

"Uh-huh." Zoe's eyebrows rose. "You talk to him lately?"

"Why do you ask?" Mia kept her back to Zoe, not wanting to appear too interested.

"Just wondering," she said. "You two have some kind of history, am I right?"

Mia turned, praying her cheeks weren't as red as they felt. "Why, did he say something?" She felt like she was in middle school, passing notes by the lockers.

"No, he never says anything. But I can tell by the way he looks at you when you two are together. Did you guys sleep together?" Zoe asked it like it was the most ordinary thing in the world.

Mia stiffened. "If you want the truth, we used to date; we lived together, actually. But things got complicated, so now we're just friends. That's all." She looked Zoe hard in the eye with the last bit, hoping to drive the point home.

Zoe just shrugged. "Whatever you say, but it's pretty obvious you guys have something going on. I'm just saying. You're not fooling anyone."

"Wow, you sound like my sister scolding her husband for the cookies," Mia laughed.

"I just call them like I see them."

And just like that, they were friends again. If Zoe felt bad about her previous explosion of anger toward Mia, she didn't acknowledge it. Mia wasn't about to bring it up, either. It was true that living with Zoe so far had been a bit like having a front row seat in a rollercoaster, pitching up and dipping down at an unpredictable speed. If she were to really analyze it, Mia might even go as far as to say that Zoe had been a bit manic with her mood swings—acting like Mia's best friend one minute and then shoving her away the next. But none of this mattered to Mia right now, for this morning she was content to cook breakfast and be let back into Zoe's world. It was enough for today.

Later, after the dishes were rinsed and Zoe had disappeared to take advantage of her morning off with a long
shower, Mia wandered out to the front steps to sit with her
mug of tea. The late morning sun was propped fully in the
sky by now, shining its warm rays down on the happy yellow
house. Still clad in her running shorts and tennis shoes, Mia
extended her legs as she reclined onto her elbows and
observed her street. It dawned on her that it had been a while
since anyone had pasted an anonymous sketch at her door.
Was it because her daily walks had scared off whoever had
been leaving them? Was this the end of the notes? With an
exploratory eye, she took in her surroundings.

To her right was a pink stucco Mediterranean house,
likely remodeled since its original 1950s construction. The
home's landscaping was neatly manicured and enclosed all
around with a matching stucco wall. She felt a surge of regret
seeing that the neighbor's exterior was much more cared for
than her own. Across the street stood a pair of two-story
Spanish bungalows, their tile roofs the color of baked earth.
One had a basketball hoop in the driveway, although Mia had
never actually seen anyone using it. These homes looked
lived in and loved; she was sure they belonged to families.
She made a mental note to meet her neighbors sometime in
the near future.

Surveying her own property, she realized the grass was
browning and the hedges needed to be cut. The front lawn
she loved so much was neglected and in desperate need of a
gardener. The large patch of grass stretched out from the
house and around the corner and was bordered by wizened

elms and towering eucalyptus trees. Although they were messy and overgrown, she was quite fond of them, because these were the trees of her youth. Before Southern California was overrun with date palms, neighborhoods like this and the one she grew up in had these beauties. Mia knew each species by shape and smell. She knew them by the way the elm rose up and out, offering an umbrella of shade in the heat of the summer months. She knew the long and narrow leaves of the eucalyptus and how they shed their aroma of sweet menthol into the traveling breeze. Mia wondered if these were some of the reasons why Ray Bradbury fell in love with the area. She'd read that he loved to ride his bike from here all the way to the UCLA library and the local bookstore. What was the landscape back then? Did he use to smell the eucalyptus and listen to the broad-leafed oaks rustle? So many of his stories included images of trees blowing in the wind. In *Farewell Summer*, he romanticized the idea of the change of seasons by the announcement of "a touch of rust in the trees." Did some of these very trees inspire him? She'd like to think so.

Today, there was little activity, save for a steady flow of cars coming and going from the area. The air was still, without any noticeable breeze, and the rooflines cast their motionless shadows on the pavement below. On the opposite sidewalk, an older woman walked a stocky terrier that pushed his nose along a thin strip of grass, searching for something good. The woman noticed Mia and offered a brief wave before turning right, tugging at the dog's leash as she went. Mia enjoyed observing her neighborhood in this state, quiet and ordinary. It was the opposite of Carson's flashy zip code with its gleaming security gates and packed-in minimansions. And it was a far cry from Emma and Tom's street that was occupied by teams of stroller moms and identical black SUVs with chrome wheels and private school bumper stickers parked in every driveway. No, Cheviot Hills felt slower and more even-paced. With its mature landscape and cracked sidewalks, community parks, and architecture that gave a nod to the early days of Los Angeles, it was a place where Mia could settle in and stay awhile. She felt at home here.

Angling her face toward the sun, she closed her eyes and allowed her mind to drift. It felt luxurious to do nothing. As her thoughts cleared, she became aware of something fuzzy brushing against her ankle. Mia gave a start and opened her eyes to discover a purring cat helping himself to her front steps.

"Why, it's you again," Mia said as she gently reached down and stroked the little gray cat that she'd met earlier. "Have you come to bathe in the sun with me?" The cat purred louder and flopped onto his side as Mia stroked his wiry fur. He felt like a tiny humming motor wrapped in a dark gray coat, warm and full of life. "I don't blame you," she laughed. "It feels good out here, doesn't it?"

The cat looked up, his ears perking up at the sound of a sudden footfall. Mia peered down the sidewalk to discover a pair of dark shoes hurrying toward them. As she straightened out from her lounged position, her eyes traveled from the shoes up to the man wearing them. Upon seeing him, she instinctually lifted a hand to her hair and smoothed it down.

The man, not noticing her yet, swiveled his head from side to side, scouring the bushes and lawns in search of something low to the ground. He was tall; that's the first thing Mia noticed. His lean frame strode down the street in swift motion, his arms propelling him forward. He wore a crisp-collared shirt that was belted neatly in at his trim waist. As he moved, the hems of his black slacks flapped over his polished dress shoes. As he advanced, Mia noticed the loosely combed light brown hair, slightly long on top and cropped at the side. Underneath a stubble-short beard was a handsome face with kind, hazel eyes and just a hint of a furrow above his brow. The frown seemed to deepen as he passed each bit of shrubbery, unsuccessful in his hunt for whatever he had lost. His lips were pressed together, set in focus, just like his eyes. His air of distress made Mia want to jump up and assist him. Instead, she remained rooted and waited for him to spot her on the steps. She observed him like this for a moment longer.

Spying her there suddenly, he stopped short and called out, "Max!" The little gray cat, which Mia had temporarily forgotten, jumped up and shook out his whole body. Mia tried to compute the connection. With his collar jangling as he went, her feline companion trotted in the direction of the man.

"There you are, buddy." He knelt down and scooped up the still-purring cat. "I've been looking for you everywhere."

Dumbfounded, Mia rose and began to stammer at the two who were now only a few feet away. "I didn't know who he belonged to," she said. The kind eyes settled on her, suddenly aware of the presence of someone other than the animal. "He just came up looking for a scratch and I was here already, and yeah, that's how we found each other." *Stop talking, Mia,* she told herself. *You sound stupid.* The words were falling from her lips like a jar of spilled marbles, her thoughts tumbling out faster than she could organize them. "He's been here once before. I recognized the red collar." She took a step and pointed at the thick nylon around the cat's neck.

Tucking Max under the crook of his arm, the man came closer and smiled. Tiny laugh lines appeared along the edges of his eyes. "Yeah, he's been getting out a lot lately. Must be because he found something better than me." He spoke with a shy manner, friendly but cautious. There was something soothing to his low and steady tone. Mia couldn't be sure if he was referring to her or not, but it almost sounded like a compliment. Self-consciously she raised a hand to fidget with her hair once more. Even at first glance, she knew he was like no other person she'd ever met before. He had a story, a certain kind of history that must have caused those laugh lines. *Who had made him laugh?* she wondered.

Nodding, Mia opened her mouth to speak, but was interrupted by the arrival of a car at the curb. The man stepped aside to make way as Zoe's usual solemn-faced driver emerged. Disturbed by the commotion, Max squirmed and tried to wrestle free. The man gripped him tighter as he looked from the driver to Mia. At that moment, Zoe, who must have been watching from the window above, came slamming out the front door and rushing down the steps. Caught in a moment of surprise, a startled Max leapt from the man's arm and ran pell-mell up the street before darting behind another house several doors down.

"No!" he said, dropping his arms to his side. Mia took the opportunity to glimpse at his left hand and checked for a ring. There wasn't one. "Sorry, I have to go after him." He offered Mia a quick, apologetic smile and jogged off in the direction of his cat. Mia watched, slack-jawed, as Max's handsome owner disappeared around the corner.

Zoe sidled up next to her, her wet hair smelling of citrus shampoo. "Mystery guy?"

Mia sighed. "What? Oh, maybe." She tore her focus away, snapping back to Zoe's attention. "He was looking for his lost cat."

"So, that wasn't the guy you saw the other day when you fell?"

Mia squinted, considering the evidence. "I suppose he could be the same person. He certainly had the height and a similar build. But like I said, that other man was so far away I couldn't really see all that well. If it was the same guy, he was probably just searching for his pet, not lurking around the house." She shrugged. "Nothing suspicious after all."

"Huh," Zoe said, making her way into the idling Suburban. She climbed into the backseat and leaned out the open door to grin wide at Mia. "Just some hot guy looking for a little pussy." Sliding on her dark aviators, she cackled wickedly as her tight-lipped driver shut the door, leaving Mia alone and blushing at the curb.

⌒

TWENTY

I need to know how many people are coming," Emma was saying over the phone. Thanksgiving was a week away and the last-minute changes to her guest list were whipping her into a snit. "Tom keeps inviting random students and it's driving me crazy," she continued. "He does this to me every year, promises not to make changes on me but then goes ahead and does it anyway. I swear." Mia couldn't tell what was offending Emma more, the fluctuating headcount or the fact that Tom was keen on inviting his students to their private holiday meal.

"Well, I'll be there for sure," Mia offered.

"And what about Zoe? Is she coming?"

Mia glanced at the clock in her office. "I'm not entirely sure. She should be home soon and I can ask." She'd tossed out the idea of a turkey dinner at Emma and Tom's a few days prior, as Zoe got ready for work. In a rush, Zoe briefly acknowledged the invitation, but didn't commit one way or another. Mia didn't want to push the issue. Holidays were tricky enough as it was, and not knowing all of Zoe's history, she wasn't sure if this particular one had any significance to her family. From what Mia had gathered, there was only her mother. No father. No siblings. Just the two Winter women who remained connected only by a thin thread over thousands of miles and distant conversations. As Carson had said early on, Zoe didn't have anyone else.

"Well, get back to me soon, please. I have two different-sized turkeys on hold at Whole Foods and it's getting too late to change my order." A paper rustled in the background. Mia imagined Emma making notes and reviewing a lengthy grocery list. "She isn't vegan or something wacky, is she? I've already got one student who's gluten-free, so I had to switch my stuffing to corn bread. Any more changes and my head might pop off." Emma's speech was speeding up, a warning sign Mia knew well. Her sister was nearing maximum stress overdrive.

"Okay, I'll ask her. I promise. What can I bring?" Mia was secretly hoping not to have to bring anything, because any time she made a contribution to Emma's big dinner parties, her gourmet aficionado sister always met her with a scoff.

"Hmmm. What can you bring?" Emma went down her list, making more rustling noises. "How about some wine? Can you do that? We'll need a good Chardonnay to pair with the turkey and some kind of red for Tom. Also, buy one cheap bottle for the mooching students. Wouldn't want them to try and break into the good stuff. Is this going to be okay with Zoe? Can she be around alcohol?" Her delivery was becoming more frenzied as she spoke.

"I will bring wine and I will inquire about Zoe. I don't know about the drinking. It may be fine. We'll just have to see." Mia dreaded having that conversation all over again. If she brought it up, she'd surely run the risk of sounding like a broken record.

"Well, get back to me sooner rather than later. I have to run. This dinner's not going to plan itself, after all." With that, Emma hung up.

As much as Emma bemoaned holiday meals, Mia knew it was just this kind of thing that made her hostess-with-the-mostest sister happy. When they were growing up, their mother had always been a bit of an entertainer, inviting the neighbors over for cocktail hour, cooking up her famous Indian curry, and displaying a rainbow of condiments on the sideboard. She would fawn over her guests, flitting around the shag-carpeted living room making sure everyone's drinks were topped off and their bellies were full. With Jim and Trudy Gladwell it was always an informal affair, adults milling around the kitchen, balancing bowls of steaming rice while they chatted with one another.

As kids, Mia and Emma used to sit huddled in their flannel nightgowns on the stairwell, spying on the grown-ups who lapped up their mother's cooking while debating foreign subjects, like the recession or the current administration. It was Emma who enjoyed studying this scene the most. She used to love to watch as the neighborhood women trickled in through the front door, making note of who was wearing what and whether or not they brought a hostess gift. She'd often run back up to her room, where she'd pull brightly colored garments from her dress-up box and parade around for Mia's delight, pretending to be one of her mother's friends.

But, in her adult life, Emma had taken the job of hosting to an entirely other level. In Mia's opinion, her sister had honed the act of entertaining to an art form. At the Hutter parties, the tables were always adorned with hand-scrolled place cards, the linens and serving dishes would have coordinating color palettes, and only the best china was to be used. Emma relished in the planning of it all, taking time to craft five-course menus (usually for a private chef to prepare) that involved things like palate cleansers and post-entrée salads. She would always make sure the florist had the freshest arrangements for her soirees, each creation never to be repeated. Emma was quite spectacular at what she did. Mia often thought it a shame her sister didn't open her own party-planning business, given the fact that it brought her so much joy.

But Emma and Tom had gotten pregnant early on in their marriage, when he was just starting at UCLA and she was helping their parents with the family business. A short while later, the grocery store sold, Tom got promoted, and Emma was expecting. Her responsibilities outweighed her dreams. At the time, Mia paid no attention and assumed it was the exact course that her older sister had wanted for herself. Emma thrived at being both a mother and a wife, and she did so with equal parts grace and determination. But as time wore on and as Mia matured, it was evident Emma had dreams of her own that had been swept under the rug for the sake of her family.

Contemplating this, Mia hung up and reflected on all of Emma's recent efforts at making the people in her life happy. Although Emma was overbearing at times and not always acting in an entirely agreeable manner, Mia had to acknowledge that Emma had helped her move on with her life after everything and everyone else fell apart. As she sat in her office, Mia's eyes scanned the room, landing on each of Emma's contributions—the borrowed furniture, the scented candles, the throw rug; it all had her signature style of chic hominess. More than that, Mia realized the designer additions were Emma's way of showering her sister with love. No matter what Emma's opinion was of the timeworn house or how Mia had arranged to get there, Emma had shown up and lent a hand anyway. Right from the very first day, Emma was there to make sure she filled her sister's home with thoughtful touches, from the quilt on her bed to the French soap in the powder room. Regardless of her busy schedule and never-ending obligations to her husband and small children, Emma took time to check on Mia, making visits and supplying creature comforts to settle her into her new life. Her sister made sure she was cared for.

Brimming with this newfound appreciation, Mia decided right then and there she was going to show up fully to Emma's dinner. She would also take a page from her sister's book and extend that same generous spirit to Zoe.

AGREEING AT THE LAST MINUTE TO ACCOMPANY MIA to the Hutter Thanksgiving dinner, Zoe was upstairs getting ready. She'd been a bit cagey around Mia lately, not able to make decisions and barely masking what Mia believed to be a growing agitation. Zoe had been overworked for the past few weeks, coming home at all hours and not eating much. It was no secret that things weren't going well on Girard's set. Mia had contemplated phoning Carson to take his temperature on the scenario, but she was afraid to face him, considering their last encounter. It was silly and selfish, but she wasn't ready to open the lid on that discussion.

Despite all of this, Mia couldn't help but feel that Zoe's restlessness was stemming from something else entirely, something deeper. Unable to put her finger on the cause of Zoe's edginess, she tried the best she could to remain neutral and not to pry. Mia had hoped that being around her family and partaking in the Thanksgiving festivities would quell whatever fire was bubbling just beneath Zoe's surface.

It wasn't until after the two of them had loaded up Mia's car with their coats, several bottles of wine, and an orchid for Emma, that Zoe opened up.

"She called a few days ago," Zoe said as she buckled herself into the passenger seat. Mia pulled her hand away from starting the ignition and faced Zoe. Although she had showered and put on a nice shift dress paired with tall suede boots, Zoe still looked ragged. It wasn't her clothes or her hair, which was blown dry and curled in lovely loose waves, nor was it her eyes, which shone amid a significant layer of mascara and concealer. Tonight, all of these elements would likely show Zoe off as the stunning girl that she was. But this was all a thinly masked illusion to Mia. She could sense, by the wringing of Zoe's hands and her empty stare out the window, that something was troubling her.

Pretending to glance in the side mirror, Mia raked her eyes over Zoe, gauging the sadness behind her voice. "Who called?"

"My mom," Zoe said, her voice low and hollow. "She called the other day when I was just getting home."

"Oh." Mia laid her hands in her lap and did her best to remain open. "Is that a good thing?"

Zoe fiddled with the hem of her dress. She looked like a little girl who had lost her way. "I don't know. She told me she and Jean Luc are getting married."

"Oh. That's her boyfriend? Is that a good thing?" Mia was beginning to sound like a parrot. She didn't know what else to say.

"My mom thinks it is. He's an *artist*." Zoe hooked her fingers to make quotes. "He paints these strange, large-scale modern pieces. Apparently he shows his work in several important French galleries. I don't know. It all looks like a bunch of big squares and paint splotches to me." Zoe took a breath, her eyes suddenly growing misty. "She says he has a kid, Claire, who's moved in with them because she doesn't get along with her mother. Isn't that so fucked up?" She threw her hands up and chuckled. "I mean, she couldn't even stick around long enough for me to live with her, yet she has no problem moving some random stranger's kid in with her instead. You should have heard her. She was going on and on about how creative this Claire girl is and how she takes art classes and brings all her other fifteen-year-old girlfriends over on the weekends. My mom has apparently been learning to cook and testing her newfound passion out on Jean Luc and Claire. One big happy family." Zoe spit the words out with bitter resentment. "The funny thing is, my mom is a terrible cook; she burns everything. But you wouldn't know it by talking to her. She's making it sound like she's mom of the year all of a sudden."

Mia's heart sank. So this was the cause of Zoe's mounting unhappiness over the past few days. Her mother, who, in all senses of the word, had abandoned her teenage daughter to follow a man across the ocean, was now setting up house with a new family. This Claire girl was benefiting from all of the motherly things that Zoe never got. She placed a hand on Zoe's shoulder. "Oh, Zoe. That sounds . . . well . . . it sounds like something hard to hear."

"Whatever," Zoe said, using her forefingers to rub at her temples, shielding her damp eyes from Mia. "It'll only be a matter of time before my mom gets bored and will want to move on. Wait and see what Jean Luc and Claire think of her then." She let out a forced chortle that gurgled up from the back of her throat. Mia wasn't sure if Zoe was holding back a sob or if she was attempting to sound sarcastic. Either way, Mia was certain that she was on the edge of an emotional eruption.

They sat there in the front seat, not moving from the driveway, for a moment longer. Mia waited for Zoe to say more, but she didn't. Mia's mind raced with an appropriate response. Should she laugh? Should she offer a clichéd quote about looking on the bright side or say something terse about forgetting her mother and moving on? If only Emma were here. She'd know what to say. Emma, with her common sense and years of motherly advice, probably wouldn't hesitate to think of exactly the right thing to say at a time like this. Mia envied her sister right then, the way she could see a situation for what it was worth and make the best of it. For now, Mia could only give Zoe's shoulder a little squeeze before turning on the car and driving away in silence.

TWENTY-ONE

⌒

*T*he Hutter house was buzzing with frenzied energy. Even from the front door, Mia and Zoe could hear the commotion of pots and pans and Emma's barking of instructions from somewhere inside. An impish little girl with pool-blue eyes and a giant red bow affixed to the top of her head greeted their knock. The girl stood on the tips of her shiny black Mary Janes and gave a toothy grin. "Hi, Auntie Mia," she said in a cartoonlike squeal. She swung the door wide open and gave a twirl, sending the skirt of her navy dress flying. "Did you see my new dress?" At six years old, Anna was the spitting image of Tom—caramel-colored hair, round blue eyes, and a row of freckles across her bump of a nose. She held her dress by the pleats and raised her eyebrows expectantly at her aunt.

"Why, how lovely and grown-up you look today!" Mia stepped into the foyer and kissed Anna on the top of her head, careful not to disturb the bow that her sister had strategically pinned. The Hutter children were always dressed to the nines when company came over. Crouching down, Mia brought her face to Anna's level and rubbed noses with her. She gestured in Zoe's direction. "Sweetie, this is my friend, Zoe."

Anna grazed her inquisitive blue eyes over a waiting Zoe, glancing from the soles of her boots all the way to the top of her dress and back down again. Zoe inched forward, stifling a giggle. "Nice to meet you, Anna. I can tell right away you are your mother's daughter." Anna frowned at this observation, wrinkling up her smooth pint-sized features. With a suspicious regard, she returned Zoe's handshake. Still sizing up this new stranger, Anna led them down the hallway and informed them that her mother was in the kitchen. Turning on her polished heels, Anna said good-bye and skipped upstairs in search of Michael.

"Geez, I don't know who I'm more intimidated by," Zoe whispered as they made their way through the house. "Your niece or your sister."

Mia nodded with a half smile. It was a relief to see that some of Zoe's sadness from the car ride had dissipated. Maybe a night with a large family would do her some good after all. But it was a bit uncomfortable the way the Hutter females had given Zoe an obvious once-over in identical fashion. "Like mother, like daughter, I guess," Mia offered. "Don't worry, they judge everyone equally, not just you." Mia gave a wink. "Come on, let's go find everyone else."

Entering the sprawling living room, Mia noted her sister's house looked picture perfect, as usual. A wood fire was crackling despite the mild temperature, piano music was piping from the surround sound, and the overstuffed designer sofas were fluffed to their full potential with a little karate chop in the center of each cushion, making the pillows resemble a row of stiff meringues. Delicate crystal bowls of mixed nuts and flickering votive candles were arranged throughout the room, next to stacks of cocktail napkins featuring artful Thanksgiving turkeys. Zoe walked around, surveying the room. "Wow, is it always like this when she entertains?"

Mia popped a handful of almonds into her mouth. "You have no idea," she said. Opening up a paper grocery sack, Mia placed the potted orchid and three bottles of wine on the room's wet bar. She had to move aside half a dozen bottles that were already chilled and displayed. Apparently she hadn't needed to bring anything to the party after all. She wondered if Emma hadn't trusted her to remember the wine or if she just didn't have faith that she'd picked the correct kind. Spying Tom with a group of people outside, she motioned in their direction and suggested to Zoe that they head out to the backyard.

"Well, hello there." Emma emerged from around the corner just as the two women were making their way through the screen door. Striding over wearing a green form-fitting DVF wrap dress, her flawless makeup only slightly giving away her tense expression, Emma received her guests. "I was in the kitchen talking with the chef; I didn't hear you come in." She leaned over and air-kissed first Mia, then Zoe, on the cheek. She smelled of figs and rosemary.

"Hi. Happy Thanksgiving." Mia returned the kiss.

"Hi," Zoe said. "Thanks for inviting me. The house looks so pretty."

Emma's glossed lips parted in an approving smile. "Why, thank you, Zoe. It's nice to have you here. Make yourself at home." Mia was grateful for her sister's welcome. Before they arrived, she'd wanted to somehow text Emma to alert her about Zoe's disappointing news from France. It was important that Zoe have a nice time tonight. Mia might not be able to offer her a visit with her flake of a mother, but she could at the very least offer Emma's little family for the sake of normalcy. She didn't want Zoe to lose faith in the idea of family altogether; the dynamic may not be a perfect one, but it was better than nothing.

Feeling pressed for time, Emma glanced down at her wristwatch. "I have to go manage things in the kitchen. The potatoes didn't get put into the oven on time and who knows what else wasn't done right when I was otherwise occupied. Can you go outside and keep Tom's guests busy?" Saying his name, she dropped her smile. Worry lines formed around the corners of her eyes. "He's supposed to be in here, helping me get the extra chairs from the garage, but it seems that his students have distracted him." She looked beyond Mia to the small cluster of guests surrounding her husband. Her focus settled on the lone female of the group.

Standing with the men was a girl who appeared to be about Zoe's age, with a raisin-brown tan and earthy-looking beauty. With her long legs and round derriere, she was the kind of girl who could pull off wearing a gunnysack and still look sexy. She laughed and snapped her waist-length hair around as she responded to something funny that Tom was saying. "Oh, for god's sake," Emma mumbled under her breath.

"Um, who's out there, exactly?" As she witnessed her sister's reaction, a lump lodged in Mia's throat. Something was off and she suspected that very something was the flirting young woman who was standing a touch too close to her brother-in-law.

"Oh, just a few of his *prized* students," Emma rolled her eyes. "He's been entertaining more and more of them at the house on weekends. You know how much he loves to use his barbecue. Frankly, I think it's just an excuse to smoke those hideous cigarettes of his, but he's out there grilling burgers for gaggles of flannel-shirted kids nonetheless. Sunday nights around here are becoming far too crowded. I don't mind, I guess, as long as they all stay outside and are gone by the time Anna and Michael go to bed." She nodded at the backyard. "But really, does he have to bring them around for our family holiday gathering? Where are their own families? I put up a bit of a protest a few days ago, but he told me that I was overreacting, so I let it go. Choose your battles, isn't that what they say?" Her chuckle had a nervous edge to it. Recognizing that she was revealing too much in front of Zoe, Emma forced a weary smile and shook her head. "Oh, here I am going on about boring marital things when you two would probably rather be outside with the rest of the party. Go on now." She ushered them out the door. "Out you go. See you in a bit." And with that, Emma scooted off in the direction of the kitchen to micromanage the hired help and probably save face for a while. Stepping out onto the brick patio, Mia raised an eyebrow at Zoe. "Ready?"

Zoe nodded, her eyes wide, probably a little stunned at Emma's confession.

"Mia! Zoe!" Tom bellowed at seeing them. Exiting from the center of his student huddle, he stepped out to greet them. With his usual joviality, he reached out and wrapped each of his broad arms around Mia and Zoe, locking them in a group hug. With her face pressed against the collar of his soft denim shirt, Mia inhaled a faint whiff of tobacco. She squeezed back for a moment, then unhooked herself and smiled at the other three people standing nearby. Along with the tan brunette was a sheepish-looking beanpole of a boy and a messy-haired surfer type who offered a smug grin. The surfer kid ignored Mia and gawked at Zoe.

"Holy shit," he said almost to himself. "Aren't you Zoe Winter?"

Mia tensed. She hadn't been with Zoe in public before and completely forgot about the effect she made on other people.

Taking the remark in stride, Zoe moved in and held out her hand. "Hi. Yes, I'm Zoe. Nice to meet you." Mia's heart swelled a little bit. Despite this ill-mannered lug, Zoe remained generous and polite. Although she realized Zoe probably had to deal with people like this all the time, she still admired the actress for keeping her composure.

"Cool," the surfer shook her hand enthusiastically. "I'm Fletcher. Nice ta meetcha."

"Um, hmmm," Zoe said as he continued to pump her hand.

Tom interrupted Fletcher's ogling and introduced the rest of his students. "Zoe, Mia, this is Lisa. And this here is Eric. They're all in my honors ancient history seminar. Top of their class, all of them!" Tom reached out and slapped a shy-looking Eric on the back. "Don't let this guy fool you. He's a modern-day walking encyclopedia of history, this one!" Eric lifted his heavy-lidded eyes up from his shoes and gave an embarrassed shrug. "Thanks, Professor Hutter." Fletcher sprang over and playfully jabbed Eric in the ribs. The two engaged in a few seconds of air boxing until Lisa cleared her throat.

"So you're Tom's sister-in-law, right? I've heard so much about you and that house of yours. Tom says you've preserved a piece of literary history by buying it." Lisa slunk closer to her professor, flipping her hair and revealing a row of glimmering white teeth. The fact that she'd just referred to her professor as "Tom" made the hair on the back of Mia's neck bristle. Was that normal? She couldn't decide if this girl was just plain forward or if Tom's casual manner had encouraged students to address him like a peer. But Eric hadn't called his teacher by his first name. What was going on here? It was pretty clear that Lisa had designs on Tom and her body language made Mia uncomfortable. Tom, on the other hand, remained oblivious, ignoring Lisa's familiarity, and went about taking drink orders from everyone. When he got to Zoe, Tom did have the decency to offer up a diet soda right away. Mia relaxed a little at his ability to be a sensitive host.

"Yes," Mia said to Lisa. "It's a great house and I feel lucky to have found it." Mia decided to let the Lisa issue go until she could talk to Emma in private. What she would say to her sister, however, she did not yet know.

After drinks had been served, everyone except for Emma continued to socialize on the patio, reclining in the cushioned chairs and sharing in light conversation as they watched Michael and Anna play nearby with a basketball. When he first appeared, Michael had made sure to present his pet lizard, a small spotted leopard gecko named Sid, for Mia to see. Fondling the reptile, he repeatedly asked Mia if she was sure she didn't want to hold him before he was put back in his aquarium. She shivered and shook her head before he ran back upstairs to secure his favorite pet. Being ten years old, Michael was sprouting before Mia's eyes, his limbs growing like weeds, his baby fat rapidly fading from his freckled face. It was sweet the way the Hutter kids looked so much alike and were miniature replicas of their father. But seeing them grow into their looks, Mia wondered if it bothered Emma to not have any of her children come out with more of her DNA. They were beautiful children none-theless, and she was sure that fact alone must make her sister proud.

After the initial introductions had been made, Zoe settled in with the young people, sharing a chaise longue with Lisa and gabbing about life on the movie set and what it was like to work with her costar Brody. Lisa had thankfully torn her focus away from Tom in order to ply Zoe with questions about acting and movie production, saying she'd always been interested in taking a film class. Zoe seemed fairly at ease, sharing in playful banter with the group as Fletcher teased the girls and Eric looked on bashfully. Mia thought it was nice for Zoe to get a taste of what regular kids were like. Not the Hollywood community, but real, everyday college kids who were worlds away from Zoe's life as a movie star. *This is good.* Mia smiled to herself. *This is healthy.*

A little while later, a dreamy cloud of mashed potatoes and roasted turkey wafted out through the open patio door, enticing the group with the promise of a mouthwatering meal. Like a man under hypnosis, Tom rose and sniffed the air, closing his eyes with pleasure. "That, my friends, is the smell of something good." He marched toward the dining room. "Come on, gang! The Thanksgiving feast awaits!"

The formal dining room was just to the left of the living room, surrounded by a wall of windows that looked out onto the small batch of fruit trees occupying the side yard. Emma wasn't much of a gardener, but she did take great pride in her ability to grow impressive quantities of juice-producing Meyer lemons each season. This particular portion of the yard was her little sanctuary, complete with sage and rosemary bushes and a pleasant-looking pebbled path that ended at a sweet little bench in the shade. Emma had always felt that her slice of the yard had a rather Zen feel, as opposed to the area that held Tom's rusty barbecue collection and the kids' sea of plastic toys. Because of this, Emma loved that the dining room had a view of something much more serene than the rest of the house. She'd pushed back the long silk curtains in order for her guests to take in her favorite view.

The table itself was something to behold. The long stretch of mahogany was adorned with a crème-colored runner and matching place mats. At each place setting lay gold and silver chargers with dishes for each course stacked on top of each other. Emma's good silver was polished and set out, the salad forks placed on the outside left, the dessert spoons and forks laid out horizontally above. If Emma Hutter were to have a second name, it would be Etiquette. Pumpkin-tinted linen napkins were folded just so inside contemporary sterling napkin rings, and squash-shaped porcelain soup tureens sat in the center of each stack of plates. In the middle of the table stood a four-tiered silver serving piece decorated with pinecones, acorns, and fall leaves. Emma had left no detail undone, right down to the handwritten place cards that had each guest's name in big scrawling black letters.

Emma walked around the table as everyone oohed and aahed over her arrangement. She placed a gentle hand on Zoe's shoulder. "Let's see Zoe, honey. I have you down on that side, with the young people. And Mia, I have you in between Michael and Anna. And Tom, you know where you go, right there at the end so you can carve the turkey." Mia took her seat and watched as Lisa located her name all the way on the far side, nowhere near Tom. At finding her place, Lisa appeared a little put out to be stuck next to the six-year-old. Mia caught her glaring at Tom and hoped Emma wouldn't notice. Emma had likely wanted the twentysomethings to sit toge-ther, but the distance created between Tom and his favorite female student appeared to be well intended. There was defin-itely something Emma hadn't told her. This didn't look good.

"Auntie Mia, if you sit next to me, then I can give you all of my vegetables," Anna said, making a face.

"You'll do nothing of the kind, Anna Marie," Emma scolded, using her daughter's middle name to let her know she meant business. "If you're going to sit at the grown-up table, then you'll eat the grown-up food with grace and gratitude."

Anna scowled and looked down at her lap. Michael sniggered into his napkin, causing his sister to whine. Tom jumped up and told the kids if they behaved, he'd go in search of the Martinelli's. That seemed to do the trick, because the kids were silent for a while.

"Well, we're all here and it's lovely to have new faces around our table." Emma stood with her glass of Chardonnay while the others took their seats. Zoe was flanked by Eric and Fletcher while Lisa was stuck across the table with Anna on her left and no one to her right. She'd been sent to the Siberia end of the table. As Tom often said, "Emma's house, Emma's rules," so if his guest was to be banished at the far side of the room, so be it.

While the table was truly picturesque and the food was sure to be a hit, Mia couldn't help but wonder who all of this was for. Emma seemed to have pulled out all the stops, and while that wasn't particularly unusual given her propensity for entertaining, she normally reserved this kind of fanciness for much larger parties. Perhaps, Mia thought, her sister's efforts were her way of showing up the likes of Lisa. All of Emma's grandeur and sophistication were put on display as a way of puffing out her chest and saying, "See, I'm the adult and you're the silly adolescent girl, and this is why I'm so much better than you." Of course, Mia couldn't be sure of anything at this point, but her sister senses were buzzing and she planned on discussing it with Emma later on.

Detecting a lull in the party, Tom grabbed his glass of Merlot and raised it in the air. "Ahem." He waited to make sure he had everyone's attention. Michael and Anna raised their sparkling cider and copied their father. "I just wanted to say that it's great to have you all here and that Emma and I welcome you to our home. Happy Thanksgiving, everyone. Now let's eat!"

TWENTY-TWO

⌒

*D*inner was served, one delicious course after another, and the guests greedily scooped up mouthfuls of stuffing and turkey and complimented Emma in between bites. To Lisa's outward disdain, Tom spent much of the main course ignoring her, instead querying Mia about the house. Glad to be part of the discussion, Emma interjected with a handful of suggestions for updating the finishings. Fletcher, along with Eric, who had finally come out of his shell, relayed humorous stories about the ill-behaved pranks happening around campus, while Zoe laughed along. Watching Zoe enjoy herself, Mia was glad to see that although her melancholy wasn't likely gone, it appeared to have been set aside for the time being. Zoe seemed to be doing her best to forget about her troubles, which was all Mia could ask for tonight. As the evening wore on, Michael and Anna tired of entertaining one another and ran off to play elsewhere while the adults drank wine and grew full and content.

Looking at all the faces around the lively table, Mia was glad to see everyone in her life getting on so well. As pleasant as it all was, she couldn't help but to wish for something more. She didn't even know what that would be other than the fact that she missed sharing events like these with some kind of partner. If only things with Carson had worked out. For all of his faults, he had always been great about being present enough to attend her family gatherings, finding her hand under the dinner table, giving her little squeezes whenever Emma would shoot him disparaging remarks. It was a shame the way Emma, or her parents for that matter, never fully warmed to Carson. And it only got worse after all of the infidelity came to light. Mia couldn't blame them, though, of course. But before all of their trouble, when Carson still made her feel special, Mia had relished having someone sit by her side and hold her hand.

Reflecting on all of this, Mia wasn't even sure it was Carson whom she missed. Maybe it was merely the idea of being a part of a couple. For some strange reason the handsome owner of Max the cat popped into her mind. The stranger, with whom she'd only had the briefest of encounters, the person belonging to the kind hazel eyes and shy smile, had made her curious. Who was he? Did he live nearby? Would she run into him out on the street again? It was ridiculous to daydream about someone she'd just met and knew nothing about other than he was fond of felines. There was just something about him that Mia couldn't get out of her head. She'd actually lain in bed that night staring into the dark, wondering where this attractive new person had come from.

She almost wanted to confide in Emma about him, but decided not to bring it up until she knew more.

"Mia?" Zoe had left her chair and was hovering over her now.

Mia snapped out of her musing. "What's up?" She had an immediate funny feeling about whatever it was Zoe was about to ask.

"Um, so Fletcher knows of this party near campus. They're thinking of stopping by and wanted to know if I'd like to come." She must have known that the subject of parties was a sore one with Mia, because Zoe shifted uncomfortably in her boots. Her eyes resembled those of a puppy dog, large and pleading, but Mia wasn't fooled.

"I don't think that's such a good idea," she said. "I'm not sure being around a bunch of drunk college kids who've likely never met a celebrity before is the best place for you right now." Mia's gut turned over in a flip. Of course this was a terrible idea. Why would Zoe even entertain such a thought? But Mia already knew. Looking at Zoe, she could tell the girl was jittery, like someone who'd had too much caffeine. She wanted to escape and get out of her head and this was the nearest option.

"It's cool, Mia," Fletcher said, his tone slick. "We'll keep an eye on her." He slung an overconfident arm around Zoe's shoulders. "She's in good hands." His hands were one of the things Mia was worried about.

Mia took a breath, summoning her patience. "That's nice and all, Fletcher, but Zoe usually requires a bodyguard for public situations. I'm not sure she'd be safe." *That's right*, Mia told herself. *Push the safety angle.* Never mind the fact that Zoe was about to put herself into a setting that might challenge her sobriety, that just a few short hours ago she was pulsing with anger over being deserted by her mother, or that she'd been so stressed out at work lately that she was likely to let off too much steam, given the chance. At the very minimum, Zoe's security should be of concern.

"Mia," Zoe said, untangling herself from Fletcher's arm. "It's okay, really."

"Oh, let her go!" Tom blurted from his seat at the table, his speech slurring and his capillaries ruddy. He'd clearly had too much wine. "You're only young once! Let the kid have a little fun." He grinned at Zoe, his eyelids heavy and drooping.

"But Tom . . ."

Zoe straightened. "Thanks, Tom." Without hesitating, she grabbed her designer leather clutch from under her seat and signaled to the other three that she was ready to go. In a rush of thank yous and good-byes the group hustled toward the front door. Breezing past Tom, Lisa hesitated as if she wanted to say something. She chewed on her bottom lip and tried to meet his eye. Not to be outwitted, Emma cut short her farewells to the boys and addressed Lisa with arms crossed.

"Have a good night." Emma glared. She meant for Lisa to be on her way and everyone knew it. Tom's eyes remained fixed on his place mat, unwilling to meet Lisa's spurned gaze. He was in the doghouse and he knew it. Encouraging this young girl any further in front of his wife would not be a wise move. He may have been drunk, but he wasn't stupid.

"G'night," he said, mostly to himself as Lisa gave up and clomped away, her cascade of glossy hair trailing behind her.

Mia stared speechlessly as she watched Zoe slip out the door. She had little ground to stand on in terms of requesting that Zoe stay, but watching her disappear into the night felt entirely like the wrong choice. Zoe was in desperate search of escape, but did she realize what she was getting herself into? Mia's stomach began flip-flopping again. She stood up and aimed her contempt at Tom. "Nice job, moron."

Two hours later, Mia, not wanting to go home just yet, sat with Emma on the chenille living room sofa while Tom snored in a wingback chair. After his students had departed and Michael and Anna were tucked into bed, he had shuffled over to the nearest soft spot and fallen into a tryptophan- and alcohol-induced slumber. Every so often he'd let out a little snuffle sound, with his head lolling to one side, and then go back to a steady snore through his gaping mouth. Emma did her best to ignore him.

"So, tell me again why inviting her over was such a good idea?" Mia was asking Emma after her sister had revealed her distaste for Lisa. Emma hadn't come right out and said she suspected that either Tom or Lisa had romantic intentions, but she'd let on that seeing the two of them together made her more than uncomfortable.

"Tom's always been chummy with his students, you know that," she said. "You've seen how he gets when he has a beer in his hand and a gaggle of his groupies all sitting around his feet like he's some kind of cult leader." Emma pushed back into the sofa and took a long pull from her wine glass. "But that tart has been here once before. She hung on to everything Tom had to say more intensely than the rest of them. She's a blatant flirt. Frankly, it's disrespectful to behave that way in my house, right in front of me!"

"Yeah, she certainly was a piece of work. But you don't think . . ." Mia repositioned herself and tried to find the right words. "I mean, you don't think that Tom . . . ?" She couldn't finish the sentence. It was one thing to think it, but it would be too awful if she actually said it out loud.

Emma did it for her. "What? Do I think that Tom is having an affair? Do I think that he's crossed the teacher-student line and done something inappropriate?" She shrugged and gazed out the window. "Honestly, Mia, I don't really know anymore what I think. And that's the truth."

Mia felt sick. This was Tom they were talking about. Her brother-in-law, her steady rock when her life had crumbled around her, her champion of all things crazy and unsure. How could he do this? He was supposed to be the good one. But now, watching him passed out and drooling in the living room, Mia had a change of heart. If any of these assumptions were true, then he had betrayed them all.

TWENTY-THREE

◞

A short while later, Emma and Mia's long heart-to-heart was interrupted by an annoying series of pings from somewhere in the room.

"What's that?" Mia looked around. "It sounds like someone's phone." Still confused and slightly groggy, she hoisted herself from the sofa and moved in the direction of the noise.

A bleary-eyed Emma, her cheeks stained with tears from spending the evening spilling out all of her marital worries to her younger sister, wiped her face and tried to become alert. "That's Tom's phone." She knew the familiar sound of incoming texts to her husband's mobile.

"It's ten forty-five at night," Mia scoffed. "Who could be texting him at this hour?"

"I don't want to know," Emma answered, defeat in her voice. She looked like she'd endured too much bad news for one night. Flicking her wrist in the direction of a still comatose Tom, she ushered Mia to seek it out.

"You want me to get his phone?" Mia felt uneasy. A part of her dreaded what she might find and the other part was struck with worry that something might be wrong. Bad news only comes late at night, when your guard is down and the world is asleep. Nothing good ever came from an unexpected call late at night. She hesitated, waiting for Emma to confirm what she was to do.

"Go on," Emma moaned. "Just turn the blasted thing off. It's somewhere in his pants pocket."

"Yeah, that's part of the problem," Mia whispered as she tiptoed in the direction of the rumbling beast in his wingback chair. "This is not cool. Your husband has officially pissed me off in more ways than one tonight."

Feeling like a spy on a covert mission, she inched closer to her brother-in-law and cocked her ear toward the floor. Detecting that the pinging was coming from the right front pocket of his chinos, she held her breath and carefully nudged Tom to one side. He remained asleep, smacking his lips and emitting a sour exhale as his snoring carried on unaffected. Continuing to hold her breath, Mia slowly slid her hand down his side and into his pocket. Her heart hammered in her chest as she mentally made up excuses in the event that Tom might wake up in the middle of the body search. With relief, she made contact with a hard piece of metal. Pinching her fingers around the rectangular edge, she retrieved his silver iPhone.

Ping! Mia nearly jumped back and dropped the phone as it illuminated and announced an incoming message just as she was pulling the phone free. Startled, the two women stared at one another, then at Tom. Time stood still as they waited to be caught. When she saw that he was still slumbering, Mia's shoulders relaxed.

"Jesus!" Emma sighed as Mia darted back to the sofa with the phone in her hand. "He's worthless."

"Thank goodness, because I don't know how I would have explained reaching into his pocket while he was asleep."

"You'd just say his phone was ringing and we needed to turn it off. He's the one with explaining to do, not us." Emma's words were pragmatic, but her delivery was slightly shaky.

Turning the phone over in her hand, Mia pressed a button only to be deterred by a pass code. "Any thoughts?" She looked at Emma.

"Try 1234 or maybe one of the kids' names," she said. "I'm sure it's something simple. He's not that complicated of a person, believe me."

Working her fingers over numbers and letters, Mia attempted a handful of combinations. Finally, after entering 5065, it unlocked. "It's your house number, FYI."

"Figures. Told you it was something stupid."

"You said it was something simple."

"Same thing."

Mia looked at the screen. "Whoa! There's like, six new messages on here . . ."

Emma held her hand out. "I don't want to know. Seriously, I'm not ready to face whatever or whomever is on the other side of that."

Mia was quiet for a minute, her eyes frantically scanning the length of the text messages. Her brow furrowed as she computed what it was she was reading. The hammering in her heart returned, this time with full force.

10:02 p.m.: *Hey it's me, we r at party and can't find Zoe. Just thought u should know.*

10:14 p.m.: *Still no sign. Fletcher says not 2 worry but Eric says some guy handed her pills. Can't find guy so not sure . . .*

10:25 p.m.: *Why aren't u picking up?*

10:37 p.m.: *We r getting ready to leave. Idk what to do. Not cool to ignore me Tom.*

10:42 p.m.: *Whatever—If u don't care then neither do I.*

10:45 p.m.: *Leaving.*

"Fuck!" Mia threw the phone onto the cushion beside her. A wave of heat covered her whole body, and beads of perspiration cropped up on her forehead. The hammering felt like it was going double-time, her heart wild against her rib cage.

As she straightened at Mia's reaction, Emma's eyes grew wide. "What is it?" The fear of finding out that Tom had a secret was written all over her stricken face.

"Zoe's missing!" Mia said. "Those assholes lost her or said she took some pills or something. I don't know; it's all unclear."

"Give me that." Emma snatched the phone from the couch and scanned the messages. Her voice cracked. "She wrote, *It's me.*"

"Yeah?" Mia's mind was racing over the possibility of Zoe's whereabouts. The manner in which Lisa had texted her professor didn't dawn on her until Emma read the words back.

"So, she didn't say her name. She didn't say, *This is Lisa.*

She said, *It's me*, which means they've texted before. And why does she have his motherfucking cell phone number in the first place?" With a burst of rage Emma hauled her arm back and sent the device flying across the living room, smashing it against a far wall. Mia watched, horrified as her sister seethed with fury.

As he was awakened in the commotion, Tom's eyelids popped open. It took him a minute to focus on the women, trying to decipher what it was he had heard. Seeing him wake, Emma stepped forward and thrust a pointed hand in his face.

"That's right, you smug son of a bitch. Wake up! Your girlfriend is calling!" Emma's hand was shaking as she spewed all of her pent-up anger toward her husband like a blowing volcano.

Scratching his head in profuse sluggishness, Tom attempted to come to and understand why Emma was hollering. "What the . . . ?"

Mia didn't give him a chance to speak. Moving closer, she lowered her voice and met his stoned gaze. "Tom, Lisa has been trying to reach you. She says they've lost Zoe. We've got a real problem."

"More like you've got a problem, Tom!" Emma stepped in front of Mia and hissed at him. "What was that little bitch doing with your cell number, hmmm? Cozying up to your students, are you? How cliché! Tell me the truth. Are you sleeping with her? Are you?" Emma let out a choking sob and fell to her knees, her dress twisting tightly around her waist. She covered her wet face with her hands and wept uncontrollably, her body rising and falling with each fresh wave of tears. She hadn't waited for Tom to respond. Emma appeared as if she already knew the truth.

This was a disaster of epic proportions. Emma was falling apart on the living room carpet, Tom was failing to snap out of it, and she was sure that all the yelling had awakened the children upstairs. Add to that, Zoe, the very person she was supposed to be watching—to be babysitting—had gone off to a party, had quite possibly taken some pills, and was currently missing in action. Zoe could be in danger. She could have gone off with whoever that guy was that had given her the pills. She might have stumbled out into the night with no idea where she was. It was only a matter of time before some weirdo recognized her and tried to take advantage of whatever situation she'd gotten herself into. The room started to spin slightly as a sickening taste of bile rose up in Mia's throat. Who was she supposed to try and help first, her sister or Zoe? Tom was clearly of no aid, and so the big giant Thanksgiving mess was now on her shoulders. What the hell was she going to do?

Ring! They all three jumped. *Ring!* Frantic, Mia looked around, searching for the ringing phone.

"That's her again!" Emma sneered.

Mia dashed across the room. "No! It's my phone. It's ringing from the inside of my purse!" Breathlessly she rushed to locate her purse on a side table near the hall. She hastily grabbed her bag and unloaded the contents onto the tabletop; lipsticks, receipts, credit cards, and her cellular all came clattering out into a heap. The phone was still ringing. Seized with fear, Mia punched the answer button without reading the caller ID.

"Zoe?" she cried. "Is that you?"

A scratchy voice answered her back. "No, it's Carson." He sounded as if he'd been asleep.

Mia's heart dropped. More bad news. "Carson?"

"Yes, sorry to disappoint you, but we've got a problem."

"What are you talking about?"

Carson sighed. His irritation was heavy. "It's Zoe. She's in trouble."

Mia practically shouted into the phone. "What do you mean? What's going on?" Grim images of Zoe being taken away in handcuffs or worse, an ambulance, flashed into her brain like a cruel series of clips from a horror movie.

"I don't know what went on earlier tonight but right now we've got a situation on our hands and I'm on my way to fix it."

"Carson!" Mia begged. "Speak English. What happened?"

"I'll tell you when you get there. Just meet me as fast as you can. I've gotta go."

"Where?"

"Meet me at Terminal 1 at LAX." And with that, the phone went dead.

~

TWENTY-FOUR

*L*os Angeles International Airport was by far one of the busiest places in all of Southern California. Its large, horseshoe-shaped campus was complete mayhem at every hour of the day and night. The outdated terminals were usually stuffed with angry passengers who waited in massive check-in lines and unfriendly snaking security checkpoints. On any given day, hordes of camped-out paparazzi filled the sidewalks, waiting areas, and parking garages hoping to catch the celebrity travelers who frequented the airport. Mia had once departed a plane at the same time as a member of a popular boy band, and had been jostled and shoved mercilessly by the frenzied female fans and photographers who screamed his name, vying for just a glimpse.

Arriving at Terminal 1, in the international building, Mia wasn't surprised to find a similar setting. Regardless of the late hour, tonight it was also insanely busy because of the Thanksgiving holiday. A sea of harried travelers spilled in through the entrance like an army of determined ants. Luckily, Emma had offered to take Mia in her car and she'd put the pedal to the metal all the way down the 405 freeway. Mia had sensed that it might have been anger and not urgency fueling her sister's furious pace, but she appreciated the effort nonetheless. As they pulled up to the loading zone, Mia sprang out and told Emma she'd meet her inside. Peeling away from the curb, Emma went in search of parking.

Emerging through the sliding glass doors, Mia stopped short. She was suddenly face-to-face with a crowd so dense that she couldn't see anything except for the backs of unfamiliar heads. Queues were doubled up and wound throughout the immense check-in area. With so many bodies squeezed together, the air had turned pungent and humid, giving off a stench of anxiety and perspiration. Every few feet, heaps of luggage were piled in disorganized fashion, and the roar of so many voices in one condensed space was almost deafening. How was she supposed to locate Carson in all this mess?

Still in her uncomfortable high heels and dress from earlier, Mia scanned the area, balancing on the balls of her feet. There was so much commotion that Mia thought that maybe the holiday had sent travelers over the edge, causing them to shout over one another in a host of different languages. As crazy as LAX could get, tonight seemed to be especially chaotic. Her gut flipped. Something told her that there was another cause for the ruckus. The intermittent hollering she'd noticed when she first came in the door was starting to make sense.

"Excuse me." Mia squirmed through the almost impenetrable crowds, receiving annoyed glares and more than a few obscenities as she pushed her way deeper into the mass. "Sorry, just trying to find someone," she offered with a shaky smile to those who allowed her to pass. Not having a ticket, she was afraid security might be made aware of her disturbance and seek her out. But she had to get to Carson. She strained to find him as she pushed even farther through the room. And that was when she first heard it.

"There's a celebrity over there! Get the camera!" cried a sharp female voice.

Then another voice could be heard. "Did you see? She's over by the windows!"

"There's a guard in the way, but you can see her if you get close enough." More voices could be heard as the news traveled in not-so-discreet murmurs.

Oh no! Why was Zoe there? Hot pricks of perspiration covered Mia's body as she began to use real force to break through the crowd. Bracing her forearm in front of her sweaty frame, Mia shoved and elbowed against the current. *Where are you, Zoe?* She didn't know what she was going to find, but her will to protect Zoe propelled her forward, in the hopes of getting to her before countless others did. Still unable to identify anyone familiar, she resorted to the next best thing.

Stopping to cup her hands around her mouth, she drew in a large breath and yelled with all her might. "Carson Cole! Where are you?" Several faces turned and scowled at her. Just another stressed-out passenger looking for her husband. Mia didn't pay any attention to the stares. Exasperated, she tried again. "CARSON COOOLE!" Her face was hot; her throat muscles felt strained. Standing stock still, Mia craned her neck and listened hard.

"Mia! Over here!" Appearing like a life preserver in a storming sea, Carson waved from only a few feet away. He was wearing a baseball cap low, paired with a dark sweatshirt. Despite his inconspicuous appearance, Mia recognized him right away. She almost wept she was so grateful for his presence.

Pushing her way through a group of people, she ran up and grabbed his solid arm. "Thank god you found me. Did you find Zoe, too?" She searched his tired eyes for an answer.

"Yeah, she's passed out on a bench over there by the window. I have a security guard blocking anyone from getting to her, but the damage is already done."

"What do you mean? What damage?" The words *passed out* rang in her ears.

Carson began moving in the direction of a tall bank of windows on the far side of the room, just beyond the blue and white Air France check-in counters. Just then, a heavyset man in an acid-washed denim jacket brushed past them, cradling a large camera lens around his neck. Carson shook his head and frowned. "Shit. They just keep coming, like cockroaches that cannot be killed."

Mia's gaze followed the man, who continued to bump people aside with his broad shoulders, hustling toward his target. "Paparazzi?" Mia gulped. "They know she's here." She didn't even form it into a question, knowing full well that the tabloid photographers and all the other LA-based freelancers were adept at sniffing out a celebrity crisis like packs of trained bloodhounds.

Carson guided her in the same path as the man and moved in defensive motion as he spoke. "Yep. Somebody spotted Zoe and it probably was only a matter of minutes until the first shot of her was snapped. My assistant found out, probably from watching TMZ, and she phoned me at home. I was dead asleep, but gathered my senses enough to call for a car and her rent-a-bodyguard to meet us just outside. It's up to you and me to get her out of here, though, because I haven't been able to locate the bodyguard yet."

"How the heck are we going to do that?" Her stomach churned, all of the night's previous food and drink mixing into an unpleasant state.

"The security guard knows a quicker way out. He has clearance through a private exit. We just have to get her on her feet."

Mia was about to ask what exactly he meant by his last comment but they reached Zoe just at that moment. A long stretch of blue nylon had been placed, along with three or four aluminum posts, a few yards in front of her, roping off the area and keeping a growing swarm of shutter-clicking paparazzi a good distance back. The frenzied cameramen barely regarded one another as they directed their ill-intentioned aim at the scene before them and fired away shot after shot. Standing in their way was a flushed security guard who was frantically barking into a walkie-talkie and doing his best to keep onlookers at bay, holding up the arms of his blue jacket to partially block the view. Just beyond him was a row of hard-looking light blue benches that backed up to wide, dingy windows. At closer inspection, Mia spied a pair of brown suede boots attached to tan legs, lying askew on one of the benches. As they got nearer, her eyes traveled from the boots to the rest of a serene-faced Zoe, her face relaxed, her mouth slightly agape. Zoe's beautiful amber hair even looked peaceful as it flowed out and around her head in a pillowy-soft cascade. Only her hands betrayed her, dangling slack over the side of the bench, half hanging on to her open clutch purse that had spilled its contents onto the gray linoleum floor.

There was something sadly beautiful about the way she was just lying there. It was like viewing a real-life art installation, an exhibit on the lonely desolation of a young girl. Mia could almost feel her heart breaking at the outward tragedy of it all. But another, more rational, side of her suddenly fumed with bitter disappointment. How could Zoe go and do this? She was doing so well and now she'd gone and jeopardized everything in a matter of hours. Mia had asked her—practically told her—not to go with those other kids tonight, but Zoe had virtually sprinted out the door anyway. Mia had gone to the trouble of including Zoe in her family's holiday gathering and this was how she chose to act? Maybe Zoe wasn't wise at all; maybe her inquisitive, cheery spirit had been an act all along and this was the real girl coming out. Was this the beginning of the end of their relationship?

A flashbulb went off, startling Mia. She turned her head and was met with several more flashes and a barrage of unnerving clicks that set her teeth on edge. Placing her hand over her face, she turned and shielded her identity from the crowd.

"Come on, Mia." Carson was tugging on her sleeve. "Let's get in there and wake her up."

Without a word, Mia ducked underneath the barrier and waited beside Carson while he and the guard discussed an exit strategy. According to the exasperated employee, more airport security was on its way to try and clear out the photographers who were now causing a fire hazard with their mosh pit formation. "You better get her out of here before the LAPD brings in riot squads, because that's what this is turning into." He was all business as he issued instructions and told them they'd better have a car waiting outside. They nodded and assured him that they did. Checking his cell phone once more, Carson indicated that help was indeed waiting in the loading zone just outside the terminal.

"Let's get her up then," Carson said.

Mia crouched down at Zoe's lifeless form and placed a firm hand on her chest. Her palm rose and fell with Zoe's shallow but steady breaths. Shaking her slightly, Mia spoke in a little more than a whisper. "Zoe. Zoe, honey, it's time to get up now. Zoe? Do you hear me?" She thought she saw Zoe's eyelids flicker. Encouraged, she upped the volume of her request. "Zoe. I need you to wake up. I'm here to take you home." Waiting for a reaction, Mia realized for the first time that night that maybe she didn't even want Zoe to come back home with her. She wanted Zoe to be okay, of that she was sure. But perhaps bringing her back to the shelter of her house on Cheviot Drive was not in either of their best interests. What exactly would she do with her there once daylight came? Was Mia capable of handling this precipitously unstable situation on a long-term basis? At the moment, she didn't have time to consider it further because Zoe began to rouse.

"Mmm, huh?" Zoe's speech came slowly, her tongue thick with sleep.

Not wanting her to slip back into her comalike condition, Mia used both hands now to shake Zoe harder. Zoe's head rolled around as she came to. "Meee-uh?" she slurred out. "What'd are you doing heeere?" Her eyes were glazed over in such a way that Mia's panicky hot flashes returned. Was Zoe going to have to be driven to the hospital and get her stomach pumped or something horrible?

"Up we go!" Carson stepped in and grabbed Zoe by the shoulders, pushing her to a sitting position. "No time for chitchat, ladies. Time's a wasting." With a grunt, he inserted his arms under Zoe's and heaved her fully upright in one swift motion. "Get her bag, Mia. Let's see if she can walk to the door."

Mia did what she was told, scooping up credit cards, loose papers, and a phone into Zoe's purse. Just as she was standing back up, she noticed a metallic wrapper of some kind glinting up at her from the dirty floor. It appeared medicinal in nature, but without any label. Hastily, she snatched it up and shoved it into her pocket for later inspection. She had a sinking feeling that whatever it turned out to be wasn't going to be good.

Another guard had arrived at this point, along with a stern-looking woman in a dark suit and matching walkie-talkie. Together, they managed to hustle Carson, Zoe, and Mia toward the exit, a firestorm of clicking and flashbulbs at their backs. Mia caught up to Carson and hoisted Zoe's right arm over her shoulders as the three of them pushed out the door and into the cold, unsympathetic night.

TWENTY-FIVE

⌐

Carson, so help me . . ." Mia was shouting in the front seat of Emma's speeding Mercedes wagon. In front of them was a darkened SUV carrying Carson, Zoe, and her bodyguard as they all made their way back to Cheviot Hills. Mia continued her tirade over the phone, defending herself against Carson's accusations. "If you are going to say this is my fault one more time, I'm hanging up!"

"Yeah!" An eavesdropping Emma gripped the steering wheel and hollered in the direction of Mia's phone. "How about taking responsibility for a change, Carson? How about this is all your fault?" Her rage was still fresh, and so was her current venom for men.

"Oh, tell your sister to shut up, will you?" Carson barked back through the receiver.

Mia smirked. "You tell her to shut up. I dare you!" The way she was feeling toward Carson, she should sic Emma on him. He deserved a little verbal thrashing, the way he was treating Mia, practically accusing her of handing Zoe the drugs herself.

Carson scoffed.

"And why are we all going back to my place anyway?" she demanded. "If Zoe is still out of it in the back of that car, then you should be instructing your driver to head straight to the hospital. Remember, we don't know what she took tonight. It could be something really damaging. Get her looked at by a professional, Carson. Because believe you me, you are no professional!" She punched End on her phone and sat seething in the passenger seat, a stream of red and white car lights whizzing past her window. "He can be such a jerk!" She flung her head against the headrest.

Her sister chuckled, giving the first sign of the night that she was going to be okay. "And you're just now figuring this out? I could have saved you some serious time and informed you of that major character flaw a long time ago."

"Ha-ha. Very funny. I know, my life would be a lot less complicated if I just listened to you more often." She slumped farther into the bucket seat and stared out the window.

"So are you going to call him back? I really do think a doctor should look at Zoe. Having her at your house could be a major liability, Mia."

Mia thought for a minute. If she dialed Carson back, she wouldn't know what to say. He could be unbelievably stubborn when he was pushed into a corner. Right now, there was surely a social media firestorm brewing around Zoe's airport appearance. Admitting her to the local hospital would likely only fan the flames of that disaster. And Mia knew that negative media attention was the one thing Carson didn't want anywhere near his precious movie. On the other hand, tucking Zoe back into her own bed at Mia's house sounded like a very dangerous option. What if she didn't sober up soon enough? What if her health was truly in jeopardy? Mia was not necessarily equipped to stay up all night and sit vigil at an intoxicated person's bedside. Despite being deeply concerned for her friend, Mia was also insanely angry at Zoe's recent choice of decisions. Sending everyone on his or her merry way and calling it a night was not the right move; there had to be some kind of consequence here.

Mulling all of this over, she picked up her phone and began to search the Internet for Zoe's name. It took less than half a second for the salacious headlines to pop up. Mia gulped as new dread washed over her. The online tabloid sites had been quick to react. Most of them glommed on to one particular image of a passed-out body partially blocked by a security guard. The face was not quite identifiable, but by the red hair and fuzzy features it wasn't a stretch to believe it was Zoe. The captions read things like, "Zoe Winter Breaks Down" and "Wasted Winter Passes Out at Airport." What followed was a series of repeat articles listing all of Zoe's past mistakes and drunken escapades over the years. The way the history of events was so readily available on these sites was deplorable. It was as if all of the media outlets had just been waiting, like sharks circling in a tank, for Zoe to teeter off the edge and drown in her own failures.

"Ugh," Mia groaned and turned off her phone. "This is really bad. How is she ever going to recover from this?"

Emma looked over. "What I can't figure out is why she went to the airport in the first place. I mean, where was she going?"

From what Mia had gathered, the airport staff had briefed Carson when he'd first arrived. Apparently, a stumbling and volatile Zoe had made her way to the Air France desk, where she had demanded a seat on the next flight to Paris. Given that it was an oversold holiday and that Zoe was in no condition to travel, the startled woman behind the counter suggested she come back the next day to book a flight. Frustrated, Zoe plunked herself down on the nearest bench and said she would wait all night if that was what it took to get a ticket. Carson was sure that in addition to calling security, the woman likely alerted the media as well. Celebrity sightings were common in this terminal, and who better to make a profit than the employees who had to deal with the rich and famous? This was all speculation on Carson's part, but he was sure someone must have tipped off the photographers, given the hour. That, or it could have been whoever had driven her there. Although many were asked, no one seemed to have noticed anyone drop her off.

"France," Mia explained. "She was going to France to find her mother."

"Oh," said Emma. "Poor thing. It's all very tragic, isn't it? Where exactly has this mother of hers been during this whole catastrophic time?"

"In Paris with her boyfriend and his kid from another marriage. Zoe was pretty torn up about it before we left tonight. I was foolish enough to think she had shrugged it off once we got to your house, but clearly I was wrong. I'd like to meet that woman and give her a few choice words. She's really done a number on her daughter." Mia shook her head. She wondered if this type of Hollywood gossip would find its way to the cities of Europe, and if it did, what Zoe's mother might say.

Just then the SUV ahead of them blinked its right turn signal and veered off at the exit for Santa Monica Boulevard. At the same time, Carson shot Mia a text stating he was bringing Zoe to Cedars-Sinai for the sake of precaution. Exhausted and relieved, Mia instructed Emma to continue on to Cheviot Hills. Carson was taking Zoe to the hospital.

An hour later, after Emma had phoned Tom to briefly and firmly inform him she would be sleeping over at Mia's, the two sisters crawled under the downy covers of Mia's queen-sized bed and lay side by side. They hadn't shared a bed in years, and somehow tonight it felt like the most natural thing in the world. Each of them curled up between the sheets and talked like they used to do, once upon a time, during the family trips of their youth. When they were little they always shared a hotel room bed while on vacations, lying nose to nose and whispering stories as they giggled and made up secret languages. Careful not to wake their nearby parents, they would stay up into the wee hours entertaining one another. Mia had cherished those times when Emma would treat her so endearingly, when Emma's older and more sophisticated friends were miles away. It was during those trips that Mia felt most connected to her sister.

Tonight, in her bedroom, many of those comforting memories came rushing back to Mia. It was wonderful to have Emma there with her in the wake of all that had happened. In turn, she suspected that it was equally reassuring for Emma, who couldn't quite face going home to pick up the pieces of her tattered marriage. In the shelter of Mia's cozy yellow house, the two women would hide out from the world and hope for a better day tomorrow.

They spoke about Tom and Carson and Zoe and the kids and everything else in between. They stayed up until the clock read 2:00 a.m., each of them yawning with heavy eyelids. Just as Mia was drifting off, Emma rolled over in the dark. "You know," Emma whispered. "There is something really soothing about this place. You made a good choice by moving in here."

"I know." Mia smiled herself to sleep.

The next morning Mia woke to an empty bed. Reaching over, she felt the wrinkled imprint where her sister had been the night before. Blinking, she checked the time. Nine o'clock. She hadn't slept that late for ages. Crawling out of her warm cocoon to stretch, she listened for any indication that Emma was still in the house. They hadn't discussed what the next course of action would be regarding Tom. Perhaps her sister had decided to go home and face the music.

Opening her shades, Mia stood at the French doors and peered outside. Rubbing her eyes against the glare of the midmorning sun, she discovered Emma curled up in one of the two chaises on the patio. A gray blanket from the living room sofa was wrapped around her top half and she cradled a coffee mug in her right hand. Mia unlocked the door and stepped out to meet her.

Emma smiled. "Hi there, sleepyhead."

"Hi yourself," Mia replied and hugged herself against the chilly temperature. "How long have you been out here?"

"Oh, a while. Did you know you could watch the sun rise from this very spot? It really is lovely out here." She reached over and patted the neighboring chaise. "Come join me."

"Thanks," Mia said. "Like the lawn chairs?"

"Yeah, Brown Jordan. Nice touch. Where'd they come from?"

"Zoe." Mia frowned at saying her name, all the images from the previous night leaping into her head. "She showed up with them one day and announced that we needed to sit in the sun."

"Huh. Who would've thought she'd have such a good idea?" Emma mused.

"Uh-huh. Well, she did." Mia shivered through her camisole top and rubbed her forearms to warm herself. "Is that coffee in there?" She nodded at Emma's steaming cup.

"Yes, it took me forever to find among your hordes of chamomile boxes. It's like you're saving up for a natural disaster or something! Thankfully, you had one tiny package of ground coffee in the back of the cupboard. I made the whole thing. There's still one more cup in the coffeemaker, if you want it."

"Maybe I will." Mia rose in search of her robe and a mug. "I think the night we had calls for something stronger than tea."

As she returned through her bedroom, a dark brew of coffee in her hand, Mia's eye caught her blinking cell phone on the nightstand. Choosing to ignore whatever incoming messages were likely waiting for her, she returned to her seat beside Emma and took a long, satisfying sip of caffeine.

"Wow, this isn't half bad," she said. "I forgot how good a cup of joe could be sometimes."

"Right?" Emma tilted her head back, letting her blanket drop a little to take in the November sun. "Thanks for letting me stay here. I just need time to think."

"Stay as long as you like," Mia said. "You're always welcome here, Emma. I hope you know that." And this time, Mia genuinely meant it. After all that had happened, she wanted to be there for her sister now more than ever. Facing heart-ache was something Mia knew all too well. It was a feeling she didn't wish on anyone. It pained her to know that Emma had to endure even a fraction of that sorrow. Studying her now, lying on the chaise with a far-off gaze on her face, Mia observed a different side of Emma. It was strange to learn that her confident, sometimes overbearing sister's marriage was fractured.

She'd always assumed Emma had it all: the perfect kids, the perfect husband, and the ideal house in the trendy suburbs. Emma always made it appear as though her life were problem-free. But perhaps Mia had never bothered to look beneath the surface. She was suddenly ashamed to realize that she'd been too wrapped up in her own problems to take a beat and consider Emma's life. As she reflected on the past months, it dawned on Mia that there had been little signs along the way: Emma's increased visits to the plastic surgeon for youthful-looking injections, her frequent appearances on

Mia's doorstep when she could have been spending time at her own home instead. What other red flags had Mia missed? She'd been too self-absorbed to notice. It made Mia's heart break at the thought of her sister quietly dealing with a collapsing marriage all on her own. She should have been there for Emma. She should have been paying better attention.

Placing a gentle hand on top of Emma's, Mia patted it softly as she spoke. "You know, I never really thanked you for being there for me after Carson and everything."

"Yes you did; you thanked me for use of my carriage house."

"No, that's not what I mean." She paused, suddenly feeling slightly choked up. "I never thanked you for all of the unconditional support. You really were a rock for me when I was kind of a mess. I'll never forget that, you know." She wiped the moisture from her eyes and smiled.

Emma returned the sentiment. "You're welcome."

They remained this way, hand in hand and side by side, for a while longer. Neither of them spoke but that was enough. It was exactly what both of them needed.

Mia's phone broke the silence with a loud ping. "New messages," Mia said. "My guess is they're either from Carson or Tom and they're undoubtedly urgent."

"Let it go for just a bit longer, will you?" Emma asked. "Let's just enjoy the peace for now."

⌒

TWENTY-SIX

"Zoe's still in the hospital," Mia informed Emma through the partially opened bathroom door.

Dripping wet with only a towel wrapped snug around her torso, Emma emerged from the shower and frowned. "They admitted her? Is she okay?"

Mia scanned through Carson's texts one more time. "Yes, I guess she's in fairly decent condition. The doctors are saying there was a substantial amount of an oxycodonelike substance in her system, but she's going to be all right. She's resting. Carson says the hospital has ordered their addiction medicine group to evaluate her."

"Good grief," Emma said. "Then what?"

"I don't know. He says her agent, Sharon, is with her this morning. What a disaster."

"So, are you going to go see her?" Emma twisted her hair into a tight turban with a second towel and leaned against the doorframe.

"Yeah, I think I will." In truth, Mia had mixed feelings

about seeing Zoe so soon, but she knew visiting her was the right thing to do. Mia needed to be a grown-up and set her anger aside for the sake of Zoe's well-being. The only problem was she wasn't sure how she'd address the issue of allowing Zoe to return home if the topic came up. With the weekend's recent developments, it was becoming clear to Mia that she was in over her head. She had little idea how to support or even manage someone in Zoe's precarious condition. And although she had Zoe's best interest at heart, Mia had zero experience with this kind of addiction. For this reason, she believed Zoe needed more structure than she could provide.

"I'm going to head out for a walk," Mia said. "Want to come along?"

"I think I'll hang out here, if that's okay."

"Sure. I'll be back in a bit." Finding her shoes, Mia finished getting dressed and headed through her front door. Out of habit, she checked the entrance for any little papers that might have been posted in her absence. Finding none, she felt a twinge of sadness. Despite their inexplicableness, she'd grown fond of the strange little pictures that reminded her of the Bradbury stories. Being on the receiving end of these deliveries had been like getting small reminders of why she loved the house. She wondered if it was the end of them. If so, they would be missed. Descending the stone steps, she inhaled the fresh air and strode off on her usual route.

An hour later, properly tired out, Mia arrived back in her front yard. To her pleasant surprise, Max the cat was also in her yard, sunning himself near a row of hedges. His tail flicked up and down upon seeing her.

"Well here you are again, Mr. Max," she cooed at him. She could hear his vibrating purr rev up as she picked her way across the dried-out lawn to kneel beside him. His fur was warm to the touch, his ears like velvet as he nudged her palm with the top of his head. Mia had encountered a lot of unfriendly felines in her day, but Max was definitely not one of them. She poked two fingers under his collar and scratched, producing an audible approval from her fluffy gray visitor. Flipping over to rest on her hind end, Mia scratched Max some more while she watched life on her street go by. As it was the day after Thanksgiving, driveways were filled with cars. Children played on the sidewalks, and generations of family members strolled together, enjoying one another's company. Mia waved as a set of grandparents went by, following an active toddler peddling a Big Wheel down the road.

"I wonder," Mia said aloud to the still-purring cat. "What's your owner doing today?" Max stared back at her in sleepy contentment and winked. At closer inspection, Mia noticed a small silver tab hanging under his chin. Either she hadn't noticed it before or it was a new addition to his usual red collar. Lifting it with her thumb, she read the engraved lettering.

Max
2223 Rimrock Circle

Mia's heart did a flip. There was an address. This was encouraging, because where Max resided, so did the handsome stranger. On a whim, she placed her hand under Max's warm belly and scooped him into her arms. "Come on, you. Let's go see if your owner is home."

Moving at a hasty clip, Mia struggled to keep a now anxious Max in her arms. Navigating the next few blocks, she jogged her memory for where she'd come across Rimrock Circle. She had a vague idea of where it might be. It was one of those streets she never included in her walks because it was a cul-de-sac and she usually wasn't interested in any dead ends. Today was a different story. Today the little strip of road had a whole new relevance; it was where she'd uncover the identity of the hazel-eyed man who had occupied her thoughts of late.

Panting now, she asked Max to please remain still as she pushed farther down the next block. At last she came to a quiet intersection, where a rectangular green street sign read Rimrock Circle. Thankful to have arrived, she readjusted her squirming package and prepared for his delivery. Freeing her right hand, she brushed a few stray locks from her face and patted at her damp forehead. Narrowing her eyes, she scanned the house numbers on a row of older bungalows and arts and crafts–style homes that lined the street. Mature trees swayed in the wind, sending a scattering of fall leaves to rush and crackle over the aged sidewalks. This section of the neighborhood had not been updated like many others. Instead, it was a charming little reminder of the architecture of the past, with low rooflines and dormer windows on the mostly single-story homes.

As they approached a maple-colored house with wood siding and neatly painted white columns, she noticed how homey the house seemed. A newly trimmed green lawn bordered the exterior, and matching red Adirondack chairs sat nestled on the front porch. She liked the house right away. Seizing his opportunity, Max leapt from her arms and padded up the front steps. Without reading the house number, Mia was sure this must be where he lived.

She hesitated before approaching. There were a couple of cars parked in the driveway, and a warm glow of light could be seen through the beveled glass window of a front room. Mia could hear some faint laughter, but she couldn't tell if it was coming from the house or beyond. With trepidation, she climbed the steps and knocked softly on the front door. Max meowed at her feet, and voices could be heard on the other side of the door. Her nerves picked up. This was wrong. He had company, maybe even a family. What was she doing? Nervously, she looked down at her faded T-shirt and dirty blue running shorts. Her appearance was less than impressive. And had she even bothered to put on any mascara before she left the house? No. This was all wrong. With a swift turn of her heel, she made for the porch steps. Too late. A click of a latch could be heard as the front door opened and a voice spoke at her back.

"Hello?" a female voice said.

Oh great. Mia cringed. Turning around with her face flushed, she offered an apologetic smile. "Hi, sorry. I was just returning your cat. Er, at least I think it's your cat." Her embarrassment had reached a dizzying level. The cat's owner was obviously part of a couple. Coming over here had clearly been a big mistake. She was met with a dewy-skinned blonde woman who appeared to be her age in a bohemian-style blouse and impossibly thin blue jeans. Mia suddenly had the urge to cover up her own much larger thighs. She took a step backward and stammered, "He had the address on his collar. I . . . I thought he might be lost." Max meowed again and slunk through the open door.

"Oh," the woman said. "Thanks. He's always getting out."

"Uh-huh." Mia wanted very badly to run.

"My brother needs to keep a better eye on him, I guess."

Brother. Mia let the word sink in. This woman was not his girlfriend or wife or anything of the sort. She had just said the cat belonged to her brother. "Oh," she said, trying her best not to sound too relieved. "Your brother's cat?"

The woman stepped out onto the porch, leaving a partial view of the house to be seen through the open door. Mia could see light pine floors and a modest entry table. The woman peered closer at her. "Do you know Jonathan?" He had a name. A good name at that. A name that sounded stable and grounded and pleasing. A name that sounded like the opposite of Carson.

Realizing she must appear foolish, she shook her head. "No. I just know his cat. So, sounds like you're having a party in there. I'll leave you be. Just wanted to see that the little guy found his way home. Good-bye."

"Wait!" the woman called after her. "What's your name? I'll tell my brother."

Mia looked over her shoulder. "Mia. My name is Mia."

TWENTY-SEVEN

⌒

ounding up the steps and into her house, her feet scarcely touching the ground, Mia flung open the front door and called out for Emma. Although still buzzing from her visit to Jonathan's house, she wasn't sure if she would share the details with Emma quite yet. Given the new developments with Tom, it wouldn't be sensitive of Mia to rush home and gab about a guy she'd met. Besides, what really was there to tell? True, there was a handsome stranger who lived in the neighborhood, but that was about it. Other than the potentially creepy fact that Mia had used his unassuming pet cat to stalk this man, not much else had happened. It wasn't as if they'd even had more than a two-minute conversation. And for all Mia knew, she could be romanticizing their whole first meeting in her head. During their singular encounter, she thought he'd paid her a compliment, and maybe she'd noticed something in the way he'd smiled at her. But did she really? She'd sleuthed out where he lived and decided that he might be single, but that wasn't much to go on. For now Mia decided to tamp down her giddiness. Making more of it than it actually was would be foolish. Wouldn't it?

In the dining room, Mia found a note that Emma had scratched out on a paper towel. She had gone home to talk with Tom and promised to call later. She thanked Mia for letting her spend the night and informed her she'd put a load of sheets in the washer. Typical Emma, her mind was probably overrun with worry, but she still took the time to clean. At the end, she'd written, "P.S. what kind of writer doesn't own any notepaper?!" Chuckling, Mia folded the note and silently wished her sister well. The day ahead was going to be a difficult one in the Hutter household.

The hours were ticking away, and Mia realized she'd better get a move on if she were to go downtown to visit Zoe. Cranking the shower faucet all the way to the hot position, she let the steam fill her bathroom and fog her mirrors as she wondered about what she might actually find once she arrived at the hospital. Carson had indicated that Zoe was okay, but what did that really mean? Was her condition just like that of a bad hangover or was it worse? Would she look sick? Would she be hostile? Mia couldn't imagine that she could be too angry, especially toward her, but then again the memory of Zoe describing rehab as a type of prison was fresh in Mia's head. Maybe Zoe was stuck on a high floor of the hospital and feeling trapped, like a wild animal. Standing under the steady stream of massaging water, Mia decided there was only one way to find out.

ZOE'S FACE WAS PUFFY AND PALE. THAT WAS THE FIRST thing to strike Mia. More shocking than the rigid hospital security, the uncomfortable IV affixed to the thin, unblemished skin of her hand, or the dreariness of the sterile room, was the shell of a girl lying in bed. Zoe, once vibrant and lively and kissed by the sun, now appeared to have had some inner light snuffed out. How this was possible after only twenty-four hours was a mystery to Mia.

At hearing the door to her room open, Zoe cracked an eyelid and muttered, "Charcoal." Her voice was hoarse and gruff.

"What?" Mia stepped closer to the bed, realizing Zoe was truly awake.

Adjusting herself against a meager stack of synthetic-looking pillows, Zoe swallowed gingerly and spoke again. "The doctors in the ER gave me charcoal and then I barfed a lot. That's why I look like shit." She had on an ill-fitting gray hospital gown with faded blue piping, its buttons unsnapped at the sleeves, revealing goose bumps on her exposed arms. Her usual shiny hair was dull and matted, her lips scaly and chapped. For Mia, this was categorically worse than seeing her passed out like a rag doll the night before.

Mia gasped, unaware of the specifics of Zoe's stay. She shook her head, causing the fringe of her bangs to swing back and forth, and blinked. "Oh, I wasn't . . ."

"Wasn't thinking I looked like shit? Yes you were. I can see it on your face. You look like you've just seen a dead body. It's okay. Not the first time I've been in this position." Zoe brought a free hand to rub at her throat and offered a meek smile. "I guess I deserve it. Nothing like retching your brains out in front of an audience to bring your ego back into check."

Mia was trying to imagine the chaos that may have ensued once Carson entered the ER with a drugged-out celebrity. The ironlike weight settled in her gut. She was regretful now, realizing Carson might have needed her help while hustling Zoe through a waiting area swarming with all kinds of sick people. She wondered if they'd been made to wait or if they were urgently rushed behind the curtains of an exam room. By the looks of Zoe's visage, it had clearly been a hard night. The room itself was cold and unfriendly, with a sharp disinfectant odor that made Mia's skin crawl. It was nothing like the deluxe maternity suite that Emma had enjoyed after delivering both of her babies. There were no brightly colored floral bouquets or happy portrait photographs on the walls here. This room felt cramped and inhospitable, more like a jail cell than a place that was meant to encourage wellness.

"You were getting sick? When was this?" Mia was still trying to wrap her head around her surroundings as Zoe laid out the grim details of her last several hours.

"Sometime last night. It's kind of a blur, but I do remember a lot of nurses standing around gawking while I barfed into a plastic bag. I could've sworn I heard them whispering to each other the entire time. I wouldn't be surprised if one of them snapped a photo on their cell phone. Nothing like witnessing a movie star with her head in a barf bag."

Mia cringed. She knew those little blue plastic bags well.

She'd spent a not-so-nice night with her face shoved into one a couple of years ago after a serious bout of food poisoning. She shuddered at the image. "I'm sorry. That must have been awful." Moving to the foot of Zoe's bed, she set her sympathy aside and continued, "But to be honest, Zoe, you were kind of a wreck. I mean, we could barely wake you." She waited for the meaning of her words to settle in. "Do you even re-member being at the airport?"

Zoe closed her eyes and moaned. "Yes, I remember parts of it. But I don't remember you being there. Did I talk to you?"

"Only for a minute. We got you into a car and you were brought straight here." Softening her tone, Mia placed a hand on Zoe's thin sheets. "We weren't sure if you were okay or not. You gave us a good scare."

Slumping her shoulders, Zoe evaded Mia's concern. If she was remorseful, she wasn't able to vocalize it. But Mia could tell that at a very minimum, Zoe was degraded. Each of them shifted under a blanket of awkward silence, listening to muffled pages on the hallway intercom and the faint rhyth-mic beeping of a bedside heart monitor. Uncomfortable with the lull, Mia opted to focus on logistics instead. Frowning, she pointed at the upright machine in the corner. "Why are they looking at your heart rate? Is there something wrong?"

Zoe sighed and threw her untethered hand in the air, a pair of papery hospital bracelets that were pale blue dangled from her wrist. "Who knows? They don't tell you anything in here. It's just a bunch of prude nurses coming in every fifteen minutes to check my fucking vitals while they try to avoid eye contact. You'd think I robbed a bank or something the way they're treating me. I just want to get all of this crap off of me and get out of here." She addressed Mia with a pleading look.

Mia wasn't convinced. If anything, she was more troubled now at witnessing her friend's pathetic condition. "I'm sure you do, but you don't look like you feel well."

Zoe sat a little straighter and attempted to brush away hair from her pallid face. "Other than being tired and having a headache, I feel fine." She picked at the dry skin of her bottom lip and waited for Mia's response.

Hesitating, Mia studied her. She wasn't sure where to start first. In the car ride over, she'd rehearsed the things she wanted to express to Zoe: her disappointment, her concern, and her slight feeling of betrayal. But now, as Mia stood in the middle of the green tile floor, all of her rationale suddenly vanished, leaving her resolve weak and without reason. "Well, maybe I can locate a doctor and find out what's going on."

Zoe bobbed her head enthusiastically at this idea. Without further discussion, Mia promised to return as she headed out into the fluorescent glow of the corridor. Finding a bank of plastic chairs, she sat down and immediately dialed Carson. She needed for him to fill in the missing details before she made her next move.

Picking up on the first ring, Carson was breathless. "Mia? Where are you?"

"Hello, to you too," Mia said bluntly. "I'm at the hospital trying to get answers. Zoe wants to leave and I don't know what to say to her. Is there some kind of plan? Have you spoken to her doctor?"

"Stay right where you are. I'm on my way. There's a cafeteria on the street level. Wait for me there." By the haste in his speech, Mia knew Carson was on edge. It was unlike him to drop everything to handle personal business. But then again, Zoe wasn't entirely personal; she was a major asset to his current film, and right now the asset was causing a world of trouble. Mia did as she was instructed and waited with dread for the inevitable chat.

She was nursing a cup of bad coffee and fiddling anxiously with her phone when he appeared. As it was the weekend, Carson was dressed casually in a ball cap and Izod shirt. Worn out from the previous night, he looked rough. His face was unshaven and his eyes were inflamed. Mia guessed he hadn't had much time for sleep. Veering right, he stopped at a coffee machine and filled a disposable cup before making his way to her table.

"Don't look at the news," he said, gesturing toward her illuminated iPhone. "It's just a bunch of crappy headlines about Zoe."

"Too late," she said.

"I've had her doctor paged," he said as he scraped a nearby metal chair across the tile floor to sit beside her. The screeching sound set Mia's teeth on edge.

"What's the matter?" he asked.

Mia had to laugh. "Really? You have to ask? What isn't the matter with this whole day?"

"Yeah, I know," he said, taking a pull of his coffee.

"Anyway, we just have to wait here until the doctor can give us an update. He's supposedly making rounds right now."

They waited together in silence, both in a thick fog of sleep-deprived thought. Hospital visitors came and went, and Mia was shocked to observe so many outward displays of emotion as people received bad news or relayed information to family members over the phone. The dining area had a restless energy, an underlying current of anxiety and fear. Hospitals were not Mia's favorite place, and today she was reminded why. Carson seemed oblivious to the commotion that surrounded them as he continually checked his e-mails and slurped his coffee refills. By the time Zoe's doctor arrived, they were both hopped up on caffeine and nervous tension.

Dr. Patel was a serious, compact man who gave a brief greeting and spoke in the clipped manner of an overly busy physician. He wore a dark blue tie and matching dress shirt with a stethoscope hanging loosely around his neck. Several ballpoint pens peeked out from his front shirt pocket in a neat little row. After listening to Mia's lengthy list of questions, he folded his arms and regarded her with grave concern.

"What has to happen for Ms. Winter is a change in her attitude and coping skills. She is an addict, and just because she's had a few months of sobriety doesn't mean things are back to normal," he explained. "Drugs are chemicals which not only change the way the brain works, but are often used to numb or dull unwanted emotions by the user. Her environment is key right now. Is she under a lot of stress? Is she surrounding herself with the wrong people? How has her mood been?"

"Up and down," Mia reported. "She's had some recent family struggles, among other stresses." Carson frowned in Mia's direction. She knew she was betraying Zoe by revealing the call from her mother, but she thought maybe it was something the doctor needed to hear.

Dr. Patel nodded like he wasn't surprised and continued, "When thoughts and feelings begin returning from the haze of drug abuse, their force and clarity can be shocking to an addict, who has in many ways stunted her ability to appropriately manage them. Early recovery can be a roller coaster of relief and anxiety and a spectrum of emotional responses while an addict begins to confront her life again."

Mia and Carson exchanged glances. Both of them knew that what Dr. Patel was saying had more than a hint of truth. Whether Carson had witnessed Zoe's "spectrum" of mood swings firsthand wasn't clear, but Mia knew he couldn't ignore the fact that she'd been overworked and overstressed. She'd been thrust back into the world of Hollywood make-believe when she should have been focusing on real life.

Dr. Patel lowered his head to review a set of folders in his hands. "I see that she spent time in a treatment facility. The tools she learned in rehabilitation should prepare her for the challenges ahead, but she needs to use those tools and have a good support system in place in case she lapses. It's going to be a long road, but if she is supported, it will be that much easier."

"Thank you, Dr. Patel." Mia stood and shook his hand. He nodded and wished them luck, leaving as quickly as he came.

Carson blew heavily into his Styrofoam cup and sulked. "I guess we need a plan B, huh?"

TWENTY-EIGHT

⌒

*T*hey huddled around the dreary cafeteria table, pushing around their drinks and slipping into an abyss of lost hope. It wasn't that Zoe's situation was utterly dire, but it was that their effort had failed. Neither wanted to admit out loud that Carson's big-budget movie was on the brink of collapsing, along with its star actress's quest for sobriety. In addition, their on-again-off-again relationship had officially flopped. The one evening Mia and Carson had spent together at the French restaurant, swept up in their old familiar feelings of passion, was nothing more than that—old feelings that remained in the past. Their last night together was a moment of nostalgia-induced weakness that had passed like a fleeting wind. Fate had intervened and reminded them that it was not meant to be.

Mia cradled her chin in one hand and twirled a plastic spoon in her cooling drink with the other. Her chest was heavy, as if something big and burdensome had been left there. Regarding Carson, who continued to sulk opposite her, she lifted her eyes to him. "We would have been shitty parents, huh?" She was referring to their mess of a job mentoring Zoe.

"Why do you say that?" Carson leaned on his elbows and propped up an eyebrow. "Because we fight all the time?"

"Well, yeah, that and the fact that we didn't always handle Zoe very well. I mean most of the time I just felt like I was treading water, trying not to drown in the responsibility of looking after a young girl. Granted, she's had some demons to battle along the way, but still. I'm not sure if you and I ever agreed on anything since she moved in."

"Correction—we didn't agree on anything before she moved in, either," he said flatly. "We've made a habit out of working against each other for a long time now." The last bit felt like the release of an ugly secret, unpleasant for both of them to admit, but a relief to acknowledge it.

"Carson," Mia held his gaze. "Was I the reason you cheated?" It was a question she'd wanted to ask for so long, but she had never really allowed herself to dwell on it without resentment and bitter envy getting in the way.

His brow furrowed into a maze of fine horizontal ridges. "What do you mean? I cheated because of me. I just, well, couldn't settle down, I guess."

Mia pressed him further. "I don't mean to suggest that I literally thrust you into the arms of another woman. But I realize I can be selfish and protective of my time. I know when I was writing the book I spent a lot of time in solitude and didn't allow for much else to get in the way. When it didn't do well I'm pretty sure that I pushed you away, for the most part. I couldn't see it clearly at the time, but looking back now I regret the way I handled things. I know I wasn't easy to live with, and I want to tell you that I'm sorry."

She sighed, remembering all the times she slunk off to wallow in bed, too despondent to answer his requests that they get out and do something. There were many times after the novel was released and sales were nonexistent that she'd desperately wanted the darkness to suck her away to a faraway place where she wouldn't have to face reality. She'd wanted to hide out under the covers of her bed and sleep a dreamless sleep, free of the worry and shame of her unsuccessful career. It wasn't that she'd wished to end her life, but she had wanted to postpone it. The lure of sleeping pills and chance of seclusion appealed to her more than anything else at the time.

In that regard, Mia could actually relate to Zoe's attraction to drugs. Whether Mia cared to admit it or not, she, too, had wrestled with such a demon. But unlike Zoe, she had come out the other end with the ability to move forward. Once she'd moved into Emma's and forced herself to focus on getting her career back on track, Mia had managed to awaken from her self-induced coma and join the land of the living. She was fortunate to no longer crave the numbness in the way that Zoe probably did. Detaching from her world had been a temporary reprieve, but she didn't miss the feeling.

Carson reached across the laminate table, his fingers interlocking with hers. Mia would always love his beautiful face. "Honey, I know it was a bad time for you. I just didn't know how to reach you, and you weren't interested in letting me try." He seemed outwardly relieved now, too, as if whatever message he'd been wanting to send over her towering walls was now free to be delivered. *Maybe*, Mia thought, *this admission will free him as much as it will me.*

She gripped his hand back and nodded. "I shouldn't have let you take all the blame when we broke up. That wasn't fair. Yes, you hurt me. But I wasn't the greatest partner, and I will forever regret that," she continued. "You're a good person, Carson. I'm lucky to have you as a friend. I do have faith that we'll both find someone who'll love us for all of our faults and everything else. There will be someone out there for each of us. There has to be."

"You think so?" He was grinning at her now, maybe partially out of gratitude that one of them had actually said it out loud—said the thing they both knew but couldn't admit. They would never be a couple again.

"I know so," she said, placing her hands back in her lap. "Who could resist your boyish charm and all the antics that go along with it?" She winked.

"And my big, fat house?" he teased.

"And your big, fat house."

The unending tension had finally been released, like the untying of an impossible knot. It had taken her years to put it all together, but this felt right. Mia was proud of herself for finally confronting the truth. She'd held on to her relationship with Carson like something to be collected and placed on a shelf, a memento that could be taken down and looked at whenever she got lonely. She no longer needed that keepsake. For the first time in a long while, she recognized the liberating fact that she might be able to go at it alone and be just fine.

After saying good-bye to Carson for the night and popping her head into Zoe's room to announce she'd be back in the morning, Mia made her way home. Coming into the still house, she traveled from room to room, casting back shutters and opening windows, welcoming the sweet evening breeze. A hint of salty ocean air drifted in from the coast, carrying with it a new sense of hope. Breathing it in, Mia had the urge to do something productive and positive; she needed to capture this feeling that uplifted her spirit. Once again driven by fresh inspiration, she found her way to her desk and sat down to write. She worked this way, in Bradbury's old study with its bursting bookshelves and musty earthen smells, until her fingers could move no more, her knuckles ached, and her eyes blurred with exhaustion. Just before dawn, she collapsed into bed fully clothed and content. Her story was finally coming together.

TWENTY-NINE

⌒

Zoe was to be released that afternoon, once all the paperwork was signed and final arrangements had been made to move her back to the campus of her rehab facility. After much deliberation and encouragement from Carson and Mia, Zoe had agreed to spend the next several weeks living in what was known as sober living. It was another building run by her treatment facility in the interest of patients who wanted to get better with some "structured support." This particular building, called Coastal Community House, was more of a glorified dormitory, and housed those who were newly exiting treatment and wanted independence yet weren't quite ready to face the demands of their everyday life. In short, it was a halfway house for the newly sober.

Zoe, being a celebrity of a certain status, was to enjoy the luxury of her own room, and could take most of her belongings with her. She was to be set up on a regular schedule of counseling and exercise and was even going to take some more cooking lessons. Because residents of Coastal Community were encouraged to seek employment, however, Zoe would return to work on the film set in a limited capacity with regular nine-to-five hours monitored personally by Carson. At learning of all of this, Mia was cautiously optimistic as she got ready to drive to the hospital and pick up Zoe in preparation for her move.

Per Zoe's request, Mia was asked to go into the guest room and collect some necessary personal items. Earlier that morning, Zoe had informed her over the phone that a pair of duffle bags could be found in her closet, along with some hanging clothes that should be clean enough to pack. Finding herself in the center of Zoe's room, Mia was pleased to find a made-up bed, its coverlet neatly tucked in at the corners like a delicate padded envelope. The contents of the bathroom were also in fairly organized order. This was a much different scene than she'd previously observed. No longer was the carpeted floor home to discarded wet towels and half-stuffed bits of luggage. Sliding open the small retrofitted closet, Mia was further surprised to find jeans, blouses, and maxi dresses hung thoughtfully in a tidy row. As she leaned to one side, it dawned on Mia that Zoe had indeed fully moved in. This was the room of a situated girl, not one who appeared to be on the run with her bags always ready to go and belongings strewn carelessly about the room as if she were waiting for the hotel maid to clean it up. Somewhere along the way, Zoe had made the transition from part-time renter to full-time resident. Making this new discovery made Mia's heart sing.

Fingering the articles of size 0 clothing, Mia considered what to pack. The last time Zoe had been in this room was Thanksgiving morning. Mia was touched that Zoe had been secretly taking care of this portion of the house, even if it was behind closed doors. Maybe that morning before they left for Emma's, Zoe had taken pains to pick up her room with a touch of thoughtfulness behind her actions. Perhaps caring for her space was Zoe's way of expressing gratitude toward Mia.

As she selected a handful of skinny jeans and graphic T-shirts to create a stack on the bed, Mia's foot struck at something with a hard edge just underneath the linen dust ruffle. Crouching down to get a better look, she rubbed her toe and pulled at the offending object. Grasping on to a hard surface, she slid out a coverless book, the same one she'd come across all those weeks ago when she'd first been snooping around. It was eggshell in color and without any detail, but something about it was familiar. Flipping it over to read the spine, she saw the title and gasped. *Beautiful, by Mia Gladwell* was embossed in dark gold lettering. Sinking to her knees, Mia was stunned. Zoe had read her book. And, although she never mentioned it, Zoe had made an effort early on after all. Mia was touched beyond belief. Her friend Zoe was still full of surprises.

Cracking open the hardcover, she flipped through the pages, fanning them slowly. Some were dog-eared, and a little star or notation appeared in the margins of others. Pointing her nose closer to these well-used pages, Mia iden-tified passages that detailed the story of a son and his father, illustrating the son's painful and urgent need to connect with his parent. Mia leaned back against the bedframe and wondered what meaning this had for Zoe. Did this girl, who was significantly younger than she and of a vastly different background, somehow relate to the story that had at one time meant so much to Mia? Had Zoe found a connection when reading *Beautiful?*

Of all the people she had first imagined would read her book, Zoe Winter was certainly never one of them. Once the gut-wrenching reviews had been published, she doubted that more than a handful of readers actually bothered to purchase the book, let alone relate to its narrative. Tears sprung into Mia's eyes when she realized that she'd possibly reached someone who needed to hear the story.

Without hesitation, Mia knew what she had to do. When she'd first wandered around Zoe's room, she had noticed a slip of paper with a couple of phone numbers scribbled on it. One of them was an international number; it had to be for Zoe's mother. Springing to her feet, Mia ran to the bedside table to retrieve the paper. She was going to call Zoe's mother and inform her that her only daughter was lying alone in a hospital bed. She didn't know what the woman's reaction might be, but it didn't matter. With a quickened pulse, Mia found the number and made her way downstairs to retrieve her cell phone. Zoe needed to know that one of her parents cared and this woman was Mia's only shot at making that happen.

AN HOUR LATER, MIA STEERED HER CAR IN THE DIRECTION of the hospital as she reached Emma on speakerphone. "Em," she said. "I'm calling to find out how you are. It's been almost two days and I've been worried."

"Ugh," Emma groaned. "I'm okay, but it's been a rocky couple of days. Tom's just run to pick up the kids from his parents. They've been on a sleepover while he and I duked it out all night. What a train wreck!"

"What happened? Did he tell you the truth?"

"Yeah, he came clean. It's not the worst, but it's pretty bad. He basically copped to having an emotional affair with this girl, and I guess it's been going on for a while, ever since school started in early August."

Mia scratched her head and frowned in the direction of the phone. "What the hell is an 'emotional affair'? That sounds weird. Was he screwing her or not?"

"No. He was very close a couple of times, but it was more of a Bill Clinton–Monica Lewinsky type of thing. All foreplay and no action. And, for the record, there wasn't any cigar in the mix."

"Gross!"

"Yeah, you're telling me. He was a mess, crying like a toddler and begging for my forgiveness. He says he'll do anything. So obviously I told him to cut ties with that little slut and maybe I might consider marriage counseling on a trial basis. But basically I'm just really pissed off!"

"As you should be," Mia said. "Is this the first time this has happened?" She was almost too afraid to ask.

"He says it's never happened before, but things with us

haven't exactly been hunky-dory lately, so I guess I just wasn't paying attention. We need serious therapy, but I said I was willing to give it a try only if he was truly remorseful. We've got the kids to think about, too, Mia. What else could I say?"

"Nothing. You did the right thing. For what it's worth, I'm furious with Tom, too. It's very big of you to agree to counseling. You have my support, no matter what you choose to do. I want you to know that, Emma." Mia saw the exit for the hospital and changed lanes. She needed to speed up if she was to meet Zoe on time.

"Thanks. I appreciate it. How goes it with Zoe?"

"Well, I called her mother today." Mia gulped. She wasn't sure how the news would be taken once she actually told Zoe.

"You did? Don't we not like her? I thought she was the bad guy in this scenario."

"I know. She's the absentee parent, but something made me pick up the phone and let her know about her daughter's condition. I did it more for Zoe than for this Patricia woman. Actually, she wasn't as horrible as I had imagined. She sounded kind of grateful for the call. I think she'll be reaching out to Zoe sometime soon."

"What made you think to call her?" Emma asked.

Mia turned on her blinker and aimed the car downtown. "Something I came across today. Let's just say I had a feeling that Zoe may not be able to move on unless she gets some kind of closure."

"Way to be a grown-up," Emma said.

Mia smiled. "Thanks. I'm trying."

THIRTY

～

*T*wo days and several car trips later, Mia had
successfully moved Zoe into her new apartment
at Coastal Community. Although the shoebox of
a bedroom didn't have much charm, with its cold tile floors
and uninspired vanilla walls, it did have a small picture
window with a scenic view of the foothills. Zoe had been a
good sport, grateful to Mia for bringing a small throw rug
and the bedding from her house. When Mia had reached into
her shopping bag and produced a little electric teakettle, Zoe
beamed. She threw her arms around Mia's neck and squeezed.
"You are so good to me," she said as she hung on. "I'm going
to miss our midnight tea parties."

Mia patted her on her birdlike back, the weight of Zoe
feeling so light against her own solid frame. "I can come
drink tea with you whenever you like," she said. "Also, Carson
said you're allowed to have visitors on the set and I've never
really hung out on a film set before."

Zoe released her clasp and flopped down on the twin

mattress. "Really? When you and Carson were dating he never brought you to the set, of any of his movies?"

"Nope. Not a one." The truth was Mia had never shown much interest in Carson's films, partly because she was always busy writing but mostly because she wasn't up for having to face the gorgeous starlets that were inevitably cast. "But I'd like to visit you. I've heard too much about Girard now; I have to see for myself." She winked. Thankfully, Girard had mellowed after learning of Zoe's recent "slip." And being the concerned brother of an alcoholic, he'd changed his tune, promising to look out for Zoe for the duration of the film. Everyone was encouraged by this recent development. It was like going to Oz and discovering that the Tin Man really did have a heart. Maybe the movie wasn't going to be such a failure after all.

After saying good-bye to Zoe and making her way to the visitor's parking lot, Mia stopped to dig in her purse for her car keys. While she rooted around, something papery brushed her hand. Pulling it out, Mia discovered a plain white envelope, sealed with her name written in curvy feminine letters. Mia frowned; she hadn't seen Zoe put anything in there earlier, but it had to be her handwriting. Climbing into her car, she ripped open the seal and read the letter.

Dear Mia,

Remember that night when I couldn't sleep and you made me my first cup of tea? That's the night that I knew we'd be friends. You said something about how an artist's mind never rests because they're always creating, even in their sleep. I liked you right away when you told me that. It's been a long time since I've felt understood.

I'm not very good at apologies but I felt that a writer (that's you!) deserved a written apology. So here it is. I am sorry for how I ruined your Thanksgiving. You asked me not to go and I ran off anyway. I wasn't running away from you, I hope you know that. Sometimes there are other forces pulling at me and if I let them, they will take control. But you came after me anyway and for that I'm truly grateful. I'm sorry to have caused the problems that I have. I promise to do better.

I also have a confession. I've read your book. I bought it soon after I learned that I'd be living with you. No matter what anyone says, it's really moving. It's "Beautiful!!" You are an amazing writer. I would be honored if you would sign the copy of my book. I left it under my bed.

Please visit me lots and this is not the end of our story.

Love and laughter,
Zoe

At the end of the letter, Mia closed her eyes and swiped at a stray tear. It might have been the single best letter that she'd ever received.

ROUNDING THE CORNER ONTO CHEVIOT DRIVE, MIA was in a dreamy state. Her letter from Zoe had plucked at her heartstrings. She had driven home recalling all of the times they'd spent together over the past two months. It was surprising how short of a time it had really been, and yet she felt as if she'd known her new friend for a long time. Life was funny like that. Some people took years to get close to, never really revealing their true identity, while other people, like Zoe, wore their hearts on their sleeves; they might be disastrously flawed, but you knew them nonetheless.

As her car eased toward her cheery yellow house, a sudden movement caught Mia's eye. Leaning her chest into the steering wheel, she peered through the windshield at what she thought was a man who looked like Jonathan walking past her driveway. His back was to her, as he traveled in the same swift lengthy strides that she'd observed the day he'd come to collect his cat. She was sure it was him, walking up her street in the direction of his own. Did he have anything in his arms? Perhaps he'd come seeking a naughty Max, who'd managed to escape yet again. No, he didn't appear to be holding anything. Perhaps Max had eluded him for the time being. With itching curiosity, Mia parked her car onto her cracked concrete drive and stepped out expectantly. In her haste, she'd neglected to properly put the car in park and it began rolling back on her, nearly taking her leg with it. Gathering up her senses, she scampered inside and turned the car off with an exasperated shove.

By this time, the person who she thought was Jonathan had exited her street and moved up the next block. Irritated and suddenly tired from a taxing drive through traffic, she gave up her quest to catch him and climbed her front steps. It was at the top step that the wind was nearly knocked out of her. There, glinting in the afternoon sun was a small white paper folded into a perfect, symmetrical square and taped neatly to her doorbell. Her mind began to spin. Who? Was that man—was Jonathan—the mystery artist? But why? She ripped the folded note from its place and tore it open to see its contents.

Dear Mia,
Thanks for finding my cat. I hope to return the favor.
—Jonathan Evers

This wasn't what she'd expected at all. Mia was mystified. What on earth was going on here?

Rapping on Jonathan's front door, Mia impatiently called out his name. Knock. Knock. Knock. Her knuckles began to sting. Red-faced and breathless, she had sprinted down her steps and into her car, coming to a screeching stop on Rimrock Drive. In the two minutes that it took her to get there, she'd repeated his name over and over in her head. Jonathan Evers. His full name was Jonathan Evers.

When no answer came, she gave up her fervent knocking and slumped onto the top step of his porch. The note was still in her hand, hastily folded and brought as evidence to prove her case. The note might not have included a funny little drawing but it seemed too coincidental that a folded piece of paper had been taped in identical fashion to her front door. What she couldn't figure out was why it was Jonathan. It didn't make much sense. And what did his note mean? He'd wanted to return the favor, but she didn't have anything that was lost, did she? Opening up the paper again, she studied the message that was written in black ink. The letters were boxy and concise, those of a careful person. Just by the handwriting alone, Mia could tell that Jonathan was not the harried and fly-by-the-seat-of-your-pants type like Carson. He was more thoughtful in his approach, more deliberate.

Giving in to the fact that he either wasn't home yet or just wasn't answering, Mia took in her surroundings. The porch, with its teak boards and white pillars, had a pleasing view. The lawn had been well cared for, with bits of loose grass clippings indicating it had been freshly mowed. The home's narrow pathway was affixed with slate gray pavers, smooth and evenly shaped rock forming into jigsaw puzzle–like shapes. A family of sparrows could be heard in a nearby tree, tweeting and chirruping back and forth to one another, busy with their day. Mia liked everything about this place. Nothing felt rushed here; quite the contrary, it felt rather comforting. Eyeing the cherry-colored Adirondack chairs to her left, she had an urge to curl up in one and just rest for a moment. But the arrival of an approaching Jonathan interrupted that thought. When she sighted him, her heart quickened.

"Hello there," he said as he came up the walkway. He was in the same dark windbreaker that she'd noticed before, paired with a checkered button-down and navy slacks that suggested he'd just come from work. Mia noticed his sandy hair and the way it was parted to the side, the longer pieces combed in a small wave at his forehead. For just a flash she wondered what it would feel like to run her hand through that section of hair.

"Hello yourself," she said half-accusingly as she rose to her feet. She saw him throw a curious glance at her car parked at the curb and she scowled. If anyone were to be doing the questioning here, it would be her. And she had a lot of questions.

Thrusting the written note in the air, she waved it in his direction as he continued to move up the path. "Is this you?" She was trembling now, the buildup of so many weeks of anonymous notes coming to a head. For an instant she worried she might appear a lunatic, but that wasn't important. What mattered was finding out the truth.

He smiled cautiously. "Of course it's me, I signed my name, didn't I?" He reached into his pocket and pulled out a set of jangling keys.

"I know that. This one has your name on it, but I've had others. Were those yours too?" She was becoming infuriated. She wasn't interested in playing games. She very much wanted this man, of all people, to be straight with her.

He paused, the keys dangling from one hand, and met her gaze. "Yes. The others are from me, in a way. But they don't have my name on them because they aren't really mine." He watched her as if he were waiting for her to make a discovery. His hazel eyes never broke their stare.

Mia stepped forward, her hand and the note in it still hanging in the air. What was he talking about? This wasn't quite the response she'd anticipated. They remained in a standoff for a long moment, she looking perplexed while he waited patiently. The wheels of her brain revolved slowly as she tried to put the pieces of what he'd said together. She wasn't sure where to go from here.

Holding up a key, he aimed it toward his front door and raised an eyebrow. "I'm going inside. Would you like to come in and I can try to better explain myself?" Without waiting for a response, he brushed past her stunned position and went about unlocking the house. He was close enough that Mia could feel the warmth from his walk coming off his body. It was intoxicatingly humid and slightly sweet, like sweat mixed with some type of aftershave that reminded her of the beach. A small tingle ran along the surface of Mia's skin as she watched him work his smooth hands over the lock. Her breath caught as he opened the door and looked over his shoulder. This was the part where she was supposed to answer back.

She forced her clamped jaw to work, slowly finding her voice as she accepted his offer and followed him inside. As she stepped onto the pine floors, she watched as he tossed his keys and wallet onto a weathered side table that held a miniature succulent plant and wooden dish full of unopened mail. He apologized for the mess and gestured to the front room. It was the room from which the light had glowed and laughter had trickled out when his sister answered the door. Mia could now see remnants of a party—a pile of pillows tossed on the floor, coasters on the coffee table, a singular dirty beer glass resting on the fireplace mantle. A vacuum stood upright in the corner, still plugged into the outlet, suggesting that someone had been called away midcleaning.

Jonathan noticed her surveying the room and offered a sheepish grin. "My family left me kind of a mess, and I hadn't gotten around to finishing picking up."

Mia eyed a child's toy car near the window. "Your family?" she asked.

"Yeah, my sister and her husband and little boy and my dad. They were all here for Thanksgiving, but now they've gone away and left me to clean up the aftermath."

"Oh, your sister." Mia was starting her nervous habit of repeating again.

Jonathan reached over and flicked on a dark bronze floor lamp. It matched the rest of the room's rustic, masculine décor. "Yeah, Meredith said she'd met you that day when you returned Max. I knew it had to be you because of her description. That's why I left the note today."

The notes. Mia snapped back into focus. That was why she had sped over here in the first place. But now Mia also was insanely curious as to how she was described. Was it in a good way or a "watch out for that frazzled crazy person" way? Shaking the idea from her brain, she addressed the issue at hand. "Right. You said something about the other notes too?"

Jonathan offered her a seat on the sofa, as he made a broad sweep to clear the party debris from his table. He excused himself to another part of the house, where a closet door could be heard opening and shutting followed by soft thuds. A few minutes later, he returned balancing a stack of books, the spines resembling a rainbow of muted hues. Mia perked up. She recognized them right away.

"So," he said, casually letting the pile spill from his arms as he unloaded it onto the coffee table. He sank down into the worn sofa cushion beside her and spoke. "The man who wrote these is responsible for the illustrations left at your door."

THIRTY-ONE

⌒

*H*alf-stunned, Mia edged forward on the couch as her knees banged against the side of the table. She winced and rubbed them with her palm. She detected a mixture of anger and surprise churning inside her, like the beginnings of an unsettling storm. "What are you saying? You mean that Ray Bradbury left those notes? I don't get it." Her eyes darted from Jonathan to the scattering of books and back again. Not all of the covers were visible, but among the collection she noted that in addition to a book of short stories, were *Dandelion Wine, The Halloween Tree,* and *Fahrenheit 451.*

He nodded in their direction. "They're all signed, too."

It was as if someone had unveiled a secret collection of rare jewels. Mia's fingers shot toward the first book. "May I?" she asked as she reached for *Dandelion Wine.* The cover art of the dust jacket was newer, less charming Mia thought, than the earlier edition, which depicted a young boy running through a summery field of tall grass. Jonathan's copy featured a more ordinary illustration of a single dandelion half-blown against a measureless periwinkle sky. In the upper right corner hung the National Book Award emblem, reminding Mia how this 1920s-era story was loved by so many.

"Be my guest." He seemed pleased at her reaction.

She was aware of his eyes fixed on her, as she tenderly balanced the book in her hands and studied it with familiar affection. Turning to the first page, she discovered the words *Ray Bradbury* scrolled in dense black ink, the *R* big and sweeping, the *y* with a long tail that flicked out and under the rest of his name. Mia traced the letters with her finger, almost expecting to feel the weight of them lift off the page. Jonathan smiled and nudged a book titled *The Halloween Tree* toward her. "Open that one next," he said, like someone handing out gifts on Christmas morning.

Taking the orange and black paperback in her hands, she paused to study the illustration on the front. She'd always loved this cover, with its windblown autumn tree full of toothless grinning jack-o'-lanterns. There were actually several variations of this image in print today. Some included costumed children under the winged cloak of an aged man and others simply featured a stark tree next to a blackened moon. Flipping to the title page, Mia gasped. "This is the same . . . ?"

Unable to finish her sentence, Mia placed the book in her lap and steadied herself. "You mean to tell me that he drew this?" Inside was a picture Mia hadn't seen before, but it was unmistakably Bradbury. On the front page of this book, along with the author's autograph, was a little drawing only a few inches in width. It was a thin sketch of a spindly tree, its leafless branches heavy with a dozen jack-o'-lantern faces scratched out in quick lines around the top of the tree in the shape of an umbrella. It was almost identical to the drawing that had been left at Mia's doorstep. "He did this?"

Jonathan nodded.

"And the one left at my door? Was that you or him? I mean it looks the same as this one!" She was talking to herself now, rapidly piecing together the clues of the mystery that had kept her up at night and plagued her unsolvable dreams.

"The ones left at your door were also done by him. Ray was quiet about it, but he liked to sketch." Jonathan moved nearer now, so that their limbs were almost touching. The combination of simultaneous events happening in the room was having a dizzying effect on Mia. She fanned herself with the book and attempted to cool her nerves. Only a few minutes ago, she'd marched over here looking for answers, but in no way could she have anticipated the news that Jonathan had just delivered. He had referred to her writing idol on a first-name basis. What was going on here? Was it possible he was a relative or maybe just an overenthusiastic fan? How was he so casually familiar with Bradbury?

"Ray? You called him Ray?" She was incredulous.

Jonathan leaned back and placed an arm over the back of the couch, his hand resting inches away from her hair. "Yes, we were friends. I had the fortune of meeting him before he became too ill to leave the house. Did you know he never learned to drive but instead rode his bike everywhere? That's how we first met. Years ago, he stopped on the street to say hello and ask what I was doing." Jonathan checked to see whether Mia wanted him to go on or not. He seemed to take her wide-eyed expression as his cue to continue. "It was a few months before I moved into this house. I was a couple of blocks down, taking pictures and making notes in my sketchbook."

"Your sketchbook? Are you an artist?" She quickly scanned the room for any signs of art supplies. But there wasn't a brush or canvas in sight, just the understated, relaxed furnishings of a bachelor.

He shook his head, sending a tuft of sandy hair across his forehead. Fighting the impulse to reach out and brush it back into place, Mia sent her hands back to her lap and locked them together. Summoning her last ounce of patience, she chewed on her lower lip and waited for Jonathan to continue.

"No, I'm an architect," he said. "But I like to pencil things out and bring them back to my studio as inspiration. I've always loved Cheviot Hills because of its untouched architecture from the 1950s. Well, at least much of it hadn't been updated until recently. Anyhow, I was in the neighborhood looking around when I ran into Ray."

Enraptured, Mia asked him to go on and hung on to every word as Jonathan unfurled his story of friendship with the late author. Always a student interested in the school of daily life, Bradbury had been curious when he spotted a young man furrow-browed and studious, examining the structures on his street. Jonathan, at first unaware of Bradbury's identity, was equally interested in this white-haired man dressed in out-of-fashion short shorts and tennis shoes riding his bike around with a basket full of books. "He was so authentically brilliant, Mia," Jonathan said. "You could tell right away, from the first conversation. And he was interested in everything, absorbing ideas like a sponge that can't absorb enough water. He said he believed in knowing about every form of art there was, and he even considered my dumb attempt at house sketches art."

A pang of envy hit Mia between the ribs. She might have the privilege of living in what used to be Bradbury's house, but Jonathan got to have *conversations* with him. She imagined the two of them, one lean and tall, the other broad and weathered, standing side by side on the street like a couple of old friends discussing architecture and art and everything else in between.

"I quickly figured out who he was, and one day, after a couple of conversations, I got up the nerve to pull out my copy of *Fahrenheit 451* and ask him to sign it."

"And?" Mia asked.

"And he did it without the blink of an eye," he said. "From there, I made the decision to go and buy the rest of his books, which I'd never read before. As time went on, I got him to sign all the copies that I owned. He was really kind about it. There was never a day when he wasn't happy and encouraging with his words." Jonathan's face drew down, suddenly eclipsed by a shadow of sadness. "Then he became too infirm to really go out anymore. Every once in a while I'd catch him being pushed around in his wheelchair, but that wasn't often. Then, one of my last conversations with him was when he suggested that someday he wouldn't be living in that house and he'd like to think that whoever moved in would love stories as much as he did. That's where his idea happened of leaving little sketches as reminders of stories. I think I offered to pass them on to the next owner and he liked that idea, so that's how the notes came to be."

"And why were they anonymous? Why didn't you just ring the bell and hand them to me all at once?"

"That part wasn't planned. The first time I did actually knock but you weren't home, so I just left the one."

"The dragon," Mia recalled. "That one had me perplexed."

Jonathan laughed. "Yeah, that was the first one. I did sort of feel like I was lurking around, I won't lie. At first it was oddly uncomfortable. But then I remembered Ray and my promise to him. I make it a habit to never go back on a promise." There was emotion behind his words. Mia suspected this last statement to be true.

Looking a bit embarrassed, Jonathan shrugged. "Then, I don't know, it just became kind of a habit to leave the pictures without disturbing you. I guess I thought of them as little gifts from Ray, not really from me at all. I was just the messenger."

THIRTY-TWO

⌐

*M*ia propped herself against the counter of the makeup trailer and leaned in toward a half-made-up Zoe. Today was her first time on the set, and she'd found it exciting to wander around and discover so many behind-the-scenes secrets of how a movie was actually made, like how many cameramen it took to shoot one angle and how much untouched gourmet food lined the craft tables. Zoe had promised to introduce her to Girard and the other actors after they'd shot her scene. Mia thought it fascinating to see how even more stunning and transformed her friend could look after some decent rest and the beautifying touches of a Hollywood makeup artist. It had been a couple of weeks since she'd moved into sober living, and by all accounts, Zoe had fallen into her dual role of dutiful recovering addict and full-time movie actress quite nicely. Mia was proud of how much Zoe had accomplished in such a short time. She knew the road ahead for her would be a long one, but she had faith that things would somehow work out for the best.

"So," Mia said in a stage whisper. "Guess who I finally found?"

Zoe bounced and squealed in her chair, like a teenager who'd just received a juicy bit of gossip. "Don't tell me!" she said. Her equally beautiful and daringly glitzy stylist, Antonio, stumbled backward at this outburst. "Sorry," Zoe apologized and tried to remain still for the rest of the makeup application. Doing her best to keep her lips in a steady pout while a layer of sheer gloss was applied over something called Plumberry Pink, Zoe continued, "Are you going to say what I think you're going to say?"

Mia smiled. "Yes! I found our Boo Radley!"

"Ooooh, Mia!" Zoe squealed again, this time causing Antonio to smudge the Plumberry in the direction of her nose. "Oops, sorry!" Zoe tried to conceal a snicker. Having had enough, Antonio threw down the lipstick with a clatter and rolled his eyes at the two women. Handing Zoe a dampened towelette, he scowled. He'd given up working on her for the time being. With a flick of his wrist, he left the trailer in search of a more grateful actor in need of a touchup.

"Oh, geez. He's so dramatic!" Zoe giggled and hopped out of her chair as they moved to the diner-style booth at the front end of the trailer. She patted a red vinyl seat for Mia to sit down. "Was this mystery person sad and lonely just like Boo, or was he something more sinister?" Zoe was practically vibrating she was so excited about the news.

Mia couldn't help but laugh. This was why she loved Zoe so much; she was always chock-full of imagination. *Maybe Zoe should be the writer*, Mia thought. "No," she said. "You've actually seen him, too. He's that nice-looking guy who came searching for his cat just before Thanksgiving."

Mia tried to conceal her warming blush at the mention of Jonathan. Ever since their afternoon together when he'd explained the story behind the sketches and his relationship with Bradbury, Mia had been on a euphoria-induced high. She'd left his house only to realize she'd wanted to ask him so many more questions. She'd lain in bed that night with her mind racing, Jonathan's stories playing over and over again.

After she left, she felt as if she had a whole new insight into the history of the house. She thought about where Bradbury might have worked on his sketches and if he ever displayed any of them in the house. Of course, she'd gone directly into her bedroom and pulled each of the drawings out from her drawer, making a plan to frame them for her den as both an homage to and constant reminder of the man behind the art.

In addition to all of this, Mia had caught herself on more than one occasion losing track of what she was doing as she slipped into yet another daydream about this Jonathan Evers. There had been the affectionate way that he'd spoken of her literary hero, how he admired his literature, and how interested he seemed to be in some of the same things to which Mia was drawn. She remembered not being able to tear her gaze from his unguarded hazel eyes and warm smile. He'd remained fairly shy, but it was a thoughtful kind of quiet that pulled Mia in and made her feel at home in his presence. She considered relaying all of this to Zoe, but decided to keep it to herself a little while longer. Just until she could be sure.

Instead, she laid out the story of Jonathan and the sketches with all the details of a mystery novel. She talked about what drawing represented which book and how Bradbury very much wanted his stories to live on, especially for whomever next moved into his house. Zoe listened intently, keenly aware that this all meant a great deal to Mia. When Mia had finished, Zoe shot her a knowing glance and curled her lip into a devilish smirk.

"So, when are you seeing this hot architect again? And don't try to hide it from me. It's written all over your face!" she chided Mia, poking her in the side of her ribcage.

Mia's blush deepened. "Actually, he said he'd love to have a look around the house and see where his friend lived. I offered to cook him dinner. He's planning to come over tomorrow night."

"Oooh, Mia has a date! How very sophisticated. The author and the architect!" Zoe was more than delighted. "I want to hear all about it afterward. Just whatever you do, don't offer to make him one of your vile green smoothies. Blech!" She clenched her throat and did an impression of someone being poisoned.

Mia snorted. Tears of laughter squirted from behind her lashes. "Okay, Zoe. I promise."

For the rest of the day, Mia camped out in a special director's chair that Zoe had set aside just for her. She watched in awe as the actors ran their lines and filmed a short scene. From what she could gather, Girard was filming the movie from the middle of the script out, leaving the beginning to the very end. The movie was a thriller about a police investigator and a girl on the run. Zoe played the elusive girl, witty, beautiful, and slightly dangerous. Mia wasn't totally sure what was going on with all the changes in lighting and blocking, but the little bits that she got to witness when Zoe put her talent to use were well worth the visit. Mia hadn't given her enough credit. Remaining in character looked incredibly difficult, especially when that cocky Brody kid would come around. He was a no-talent in Mia's opinion, but she supposed he was cast to please a certain demographic. For Zoe's sake, and for Carson's too, for that matter, Mia hoped the movie would be a box-office success.

As the filming wound down for the afternoon, Mia waited in her chair for Zoe to change into street clothes so she could drive her back to Coastal Community. As she sat idle, she picked up her phone and punched out a text to Carson. Without much detail, she told him she might have something of interest for him and asked if they could have an official "meeting." He dinged back in less than three minutes with an enthusiastic *Yes!* They messaged back and forth and set a date for later that week. He'd wanted to know what it was about, but Mia told him to be patient and she'd explain when she saw him. She put her phone away and quietly plotted to herself until Zoe was ready to go.

On the ride home, Zoe rubbed at her eyes and admitted she was tired from the day of work but that it was good to be worn out from something that she still loved to do. Although she was low on energy, she wasn't depleted in the story department. As they made their way down the 405 freeway, Zoe entertained Mia with funny little anecdotes and updates about life among the other residents at the halfway house. For the most part, she appeared to be finding her way in her new situation.

"Did I tell you my mom called?" Zoe asked, rather out of the blue.

Mia gulped and tried to act casual. She'd been wondering when and if she'd ever hear about this. But since Zoe hadn't mentioned it before, she'd figured nothing positive had come of her reaching out to Zoe's mother. "Really? She did? When did that happen?"

"About a week ago. Don't act so surprised, by the way. She already narked you out for calling her and letting her know I'd been in the hospital." Zoe was looking right at her now, as Mia tried in vain to keep her eyes forward and brace for whatever hostility might be thrown her way.

Mia cleared her throat, buying time to gauge Zoe's reaction. "Oh, yeah," Mia said slowly. "I meant to tell you. I just thought maybe a family member should know where you were. That's all. I hope you're not mad."

Surprisingly, Zoe's reaction was sunnier than she'd expected. "It's okay. I know you were only trying to help. It actually was a pretty good conversation. I'd just come from one of my therapy sessions when she rang. I must have been feeling pretty open, because I got up the guts to address a couple of things with her that had been bugging me. We wound up talking on the phone for like, two hours. It was cool, actually."

Mia relaxed her grip on the wheel. "Wow, Zoe, that's amazing. I'm really happy for you."

"Don't get me wrong; we still have our differences and she's never going to be able to make up for lost time. But she said she'd like to work on things. She even offered to have me come visit her in Paris after the movie wraps in the summer."

Slightly shocked, Mia threw her a sidelong glance. "Really? To France? And what did you say to that?"

Zoe grinned. "I told her I'd think about it, but that I'd probably only be able to come if my friend, Mia Gladwell, came with me."

Mia's mouth hung open. "Zoe! You didn't."

"Yep. I sure did." Zoe moved in her seat to face Mia, addressing her with a more sincere tone. "Will you think about it? I don't know if I could do something that major on my own right now. Having you there would be . . . well . . . it would be amazing. I know it's asking a lot, but I would buy your ticket. It might be really fun to run around 'Gay Paree' together. Please tell me you'll think about it."

What could Mia say? Something like this had never crossed her mind when she'd dialed Zoe's mother and urged her to touch base with her kid. Why would Zoe want Mia to be the one accompanying her on a trip to Europe and not one of her younger, hipper friends? But Mia thought she probably knew why. Because most of Zoe's friends were all from before rehab. They were all still living the life that she was now trying desperately to avoid. With Mia as a traveling companion there probably came a sense of security. Zoe might anticipate she'd be looked after if things were to go sideways with her mother. It touched Mia that Zoe would consider a trip to the fashion capital of the world with a boring old tea-drinking gal like herself.

Letting silence fill the space for a minute, Mia mulled over the idea in her head. As she did this, she could practically feel the weight of Zoe's anticipation bearing down on her from across the car. Finally, as they made the turn for Zoe's building, Mia caved. "Okay, I'll think about it."

"Hooray!" Zoe gripped Mia's arm with both hands, clutching it the rest of the way home.

THRITY-THREE

⌒

*H*overing over her ancient, colossal-sized computer printer, Mia tapped her foot impatiently. The machine gurgled and spit out printed pages in sporadic coughs, like a sick animal. Mia willed the relic to go on as she checked the clock on her desk for the third time in two minutes. She didn't want to be late for her meeting.

She'd been alert for hours, having risen with the sun and starting her day with her tennis shoes and a lengthy walk. This had become her routine over the past month since Zoe had moved out. Mia had come to treasure her mornings when she could move swiftly through the damp streets just as dawn broke and shed its pastel light on her neighborhood. On this particular morning, several houses were still illuminated, strands of red and green Christmas lights having been forgotten and left to twinkle and glow throughout the night. The holiday was only a few short days away, and Mia was looking forward to spending it with her family. As she moved at a steady pace, she ticked off the items of her grocery list in her head. She was preparing to host Christmas dinner at her house this year and wanted her inaugural hosting to be something special. It was a privilege to be the one opening her home this time around and she wanted to get it right.

Things at the Hutter household had been stressful lately, but holding together, according to Emma. In an attempt to follow the advice of her therapist and be less controlling and "let things go," her sister wasn't planning to host a big extravagant holiday at her house this year. Mia jumped in and offered to cook—at least order all the fixings from Whole Foods—and have everyone gather at her house instead. Emma, Tom, Michael, Anna, and even Zoe were all planning to spend Christmas day at her house. Mia had invited her parents as well, but they'd already booked some kind of senior cruise to the Caribbean with several of their new friends. They promised to come for the holidays the following year.

Now, back from her walk, showered and dressed in a polished navy pantsuit and heels, Mia set all her holiday planning aside, banging on the printer and begging it to move faster as she prepared for her meeting downtown. At last, a neat stack of pages stood like a gleaming white tower of hope on top of her desk. Mia ran her hand down the side of what had been many months worth of work, now condensed into a few hundred pages of type. With her hand on the final product, she glanced over at the little black and white framed photo of Bradbury that rested on her shelf and nodded. "Here we go," she said to the image. Scooping the pages into her leather tote bag, she snatched her car keys and hustled out the front door.

As she entered the bustling offices of Envision Entertainment, Mia's whole body buzzed like a charged battery. Today's meeting was going to be much different from her last. This time around, she hoped to surprise Carson rather than the other way around. In fact, she planned on dazzling him. But that didn't stop her nerves from feeling exposed. When she heard the office assistant announce her arrival into the intercom, Mia's already swift pulse went into double time. Taking a moment to calm herself, she smoothed the front of her blazer and nodded at the assistant as she made her way into Carson's office. As usual, he sat perched in wait behind his beast of a desk, like some kind of royalty receiving his subjects.

"Well, well." He stood and grinned. "Aren't we looking very professional this morning?" He cocked his head at Mia's businesslike manner and strode around to kiss her rouged cheek. "I'm starting to feel underdressed here." In typical fashion, he was in a button-down and dark-washed jeans, looking sharp but still untucked.

Mia returned the kiss then settled into an armchair. "I'm here in an official capacity, Mr. Cole." She beamed at him.

He lowered into a swivel chair opposite of hers and rubbed his hands together. "Excellent!" He leaned forward and peered at the mound of gleaming white paper poking out from the inside of her leather tote. His eyes widened. "Now what's this all about?"

Mia sighed and smacked him away. "Is this how you are with all your big important exec meetings?" He was still incorrigible. But they were in a good place now and they both knew it. It had taken them four years of pushing and pulling and a lot of tears in between, but Carson and Mia were finally what they were meant to be all along, close friends. And, after today, Mia hoped maybe even working partners.

"This is much more fun than most of the other meetings I take, trust me. Now, give it up. What's in the bag already?" He inched forward and made for her things.

She beat him to it and retrieved the stack, letting it come to rest on the coffee table between them with a dramatic thud. Pleased with its notable effect, she leaned back and waited for a reaction.

"A new book?" He stared, slightly puzzled.

Mia shook her head, the curled edges of her hair sweeping her shoulders. "I'm wondering if it might be more, but I'm not sure. This is something new. I need you to tell me what you think. I'm looking for your honest feedback, Carson." She had to be serious now; this next step in her career was no game.

He reached forward. "May I?" he asked, pulling the top sheet into view.

"Be my guest," she said, pushing down a slight welling of fear. "That's the synopsis."

He took his time, his eyes roaming from line to line as he read the entire page. After a minute, he stopped, looking up at her with an expression Mia couldn't quite read, and went back to reading it all over again. Finally, after five excruciatingly long minutes, he met her waiting gaze and held the page in the air. "Is this a novel or a screenplay?"

She inhaled. "I don't really know. I was hoping for you to tell me."

He seized another handful of pages and knit his brows together as he continued reading. Every so often he'd scratch his head and emit a little "hmmm," only to keep going.

For Mia, it was torturous to witness, as she crossed and recrossed her legs and kicked her heel in impatient little circles. She did her best not to break his concentration, but it was difficult to sit still while he scrutinized the sum total of her labor. In his hands was the very product of months of finger-numbing work, all boiled down to a few hundred pages. Secretly, Mia hoped it was her best writing yet, but she was far too close to it, too caught up in the setting and the characters to know if it had any real merit. Of course it was something quite meaningful to her, but what kind of meaning it would have to the outside world remained a mystery. Until today.

Breaking her train of thought, Carson burst out, "Mia, this is science fiction! You don't even write science fiction, do you?" He was enthusiastic and perplexed at the same time, but there was an undeniable glint in his eye that Mia recognized as excitement.

"I'd like to think of it as 'fantasy,' but you can call it whatever you want. I didn't know if I could write in this genre either, but it just sort of happened." Her speech was speeding up now, catching up with Carson's energy.

"Fantasy? Like *Lord of the Rings?*" he asked.

"Something like that. I was also thinking it could be more for the young adult crowd. You know, less violence and more story world." She could see that he was nodding, catching on.

"And this main character, this girl." He pointed to the page as he squinted to reread something. "She reminds me of—"

Mia cut him off. "She reminds you of Zoe, right? Me too. I thought she'd be perfect to play that role."

"So this *is* a screenplay!" Carson leapt to his feet, causing the floor of his office to shake as he waved a sheet of paper around like a flag. It was as if he'd just summited a mountain and declared victory. "Mia! This is totally surprising. But I can see it, just from the intro here, that it could be developed into something real!" He was pacing now, the gears in his movie-producer mind turning at full tilt. Mia watched as his excitement gained momentum.

"Do you really think so?" His declaration had made her a little woozy. "I honestly started out to create a novel, but the more I got into it and the more I thought about what I really wanted, the more it felt like a film and not just a book."

Too enthused to sit down again, Carson leaned on the front of his desk and addressed her. "Could I have some time with this?" He gestured to her work. "I need to digest it and think about where this would fit. But I already have some ideas. We'd need to pair you with one of my screenwriters, someone who could walk you through the process and help you develop it. But it would be work, Mia. I'm talking clear-your-calendar-and-plan-on-some-serious-dedication—a new kind of craft. How does that all sound?"

Mia's head was already bobbing. This was exactly the reaction she'd been hoping for, to find out that all of her hard work had some merit. She was giddy. "Yes, of course. I'm in."

Carson dashed to the other side of his desk and proceeded to bang out a note on his laptop. He kept talking to her while he frantically hunted and pecked at the keyboard with his index fingers. "I'll need an electronic file, too, so I can run this by one of my writers." He stopped his frantic typing and lifted his face to meet hers. "But Mia, I'm already impressed. Get ready to be very busy!"

As she drove home, Mia's cheeks were practically sore from the force of her smile. She had cautiously hoped for Carson to be encouraging, but she honestly hadn't expected for such an overwhelming response. If this worked out, she would be part of something bigger than anything she'd ever attempted before. And, fingers crossed, Zoe would get something out of it, too. Of course, starting out, Mia had never considered where her story might lead. But as time went on and words filled pages, she started to recognize pieces of Zoe and Bradbury and a stronger version of her own voice in her work. She'd opened up and allowed herself to be influenced by what moved her, and out of it was born something entirely new. She hadn't shared this with anyone except Carson. There had been days that she'd been so pumped up about something she'd written that she wanted to confide in her sister or Zoe or someone just to have them feel the same excitement. But her common sense had always won over on those days and caused her to keep her head down and keep moving ahead. She'd kept on writing until she knew it was truly done.

Pulling into her driveway, Mia now thought of the one person with whom she'd most wanted to share her news. And she knew, undeniably, that person was Jonathan.

THIRTY-FOUR

〜

On December twenty-fifth, the yellow house on Cheviot Drive was bursting with activity. Michael and Anna skipped around the dining room, snapping apart brightly wrapped Christmas crackers like paper wishbones, sending miniature spinning tops, fortunes, and paper crowns flying in all directions. Their giggles of surprise reverberated off the walls and echoed into the corridors. In the tiny blue kitchen, a cloud of powdery white flour dust was sent through the air as Zoe showed off her new baking skills, kneading out dough and chattering a mile a minute while a rather relaxed Emma looked on with a glass of wine. On the front steps outside was a very determined Tom, balancing on Mia's wobbly stepstool with a string of white lights in one hand and a menacing-looking staple gun in the other. Even though it was already Christmas day and the festivities had begun, her brother-in-law insisted on hanging holiday lights at the entrance of the house. He proclaimed that it made him feel useful, but Mia suspected it was his small way of thanking her for standing by while he and Emma navigated their way through a rough patch.

A delightful aroma of brown sugar drifted through the house as the glazed ham warmed in the oven. Mia circled her new drop-leaf farm table, setting out silverware and lighting votive candles. She was pleased how the new addition to her house, adorned with jolly red place mats and bouquets of white roses, had enough room for her whole family to gather together and celebrate. In the time since she'd moved into the Bradbury house, she hadn't filled it with too many objects, but looking around at all the happy faces today, she realized she had filled it with something much more important. No longer did she feel she was living in the shadow of another family's spirit. It was her life that had taken up residency, and to her delight, it had morphed into something quite lovely.

It was the end of a year, but to Mia it felt like the start of everything. So much had happened since that first day when she'd pulled out the worn key and stepped into the old house. She had been determined to make something new of her life. But she had no way of knowing where it all would lead. Now, leaning up against a windowpane, she looked out onto the street below and reflected on how much she'd gained since she'd purchased the house the previous fall. Her life now included Zoe, who had imprinted Mia's heart forever with her unbreakable spirit and tender friendship.

After so much time, Mia had come to understand that the job of a good sibling was not a one-way street. It was possible for the strong bonds of sisterhood to be tested and still hold together through it all. And now it was her turn to be strong for Emma.

Mia's sense of self had been altered, too. She had discovered how to allow her art to be challenged in new ways. Just because one rung in the creative ladder had been pulled out from under her didn't mean she couldn't reinvent who she was as a writer and move on from that. Never in her wildest dreams would she have imagined that one day she'd be working for Carson, developing a screenplay alongside other talented writers, with the goal of producing a big-budget movie. The experience had only just begun and she was not impervious to making mistakes, but Mia was already finding it terribly rewarding.

As she gazed out the window and waited for her final guest to arrive, it was not lost on Mia how the simple act of following her heart and buying the house had created a domino effect on everything else in her life. Spotting whom she was waiting for, Mia waved and then ran with eager feet to throw open the front door.

Tom had beaten her to it and was already gripping Jonathan's hand. As he welcomed the last guest inside, Mia emerged, breathless and beaming.

Tom boomed, "So you're the famous Jonathan we've heard so much about!" Her gregarious brother-in-law was already slapping Jonathan on the back, embarrassing him as if he were one of Mia's teenage prom dates.

"Tom!" Mia reached past to grab Jonathan's arm. Feeling the touch of him still gave her goose bumps. Jonathan offered a shy smile in return as he said hello to Tom and presented Mia with a bouquet of lilies.

"They're beautiful," she said, taking the flowers and his

hand. She held on tight and led him through the house and into the kitchen. Although he'd been at her place several times now, he'd yet to meet Mia's family. In the past four weeks, the two had spent a significant amount of time together, enjoying dinner out, attending local art openings, and even taking a day trip up the coast to share a picnic on the beaches of Santa Barbara. Every minute Mia spent with Jonathan she felt like pinching herself. It wasn't that things were too good to be true, but more that it all felt so *right*. The more she'd gotten to know him, the more down-to-earth and smart and loving she realized he was. Plus, she found his work fascinating and could listen for hours, as he would point out the architectural aspects of different structures and why each one held a specific purpose. Jonathan had a quiet passion that Mia found attractive. The fact that he was easy on the eyes was a bonus. Now that her family surrounded them and they were no longer alone, it was all she could do to keep her hands to herself.

In a bustle of hand pumping and boisterous voices, introductions were made and drinks were poured. Everyone gathered in Mia's kitchen, leaning up against warm appliances and one another.

"So, Jonathan," Emma said, sidling up next to her sister's date. "Mia says you can't stay for dinner. Are you sure we can't twist your arm?" Mia could tell Emma approved of this new person by the way she was unabashedly grinning at him.

"Yeah, Jonathan," Zoe interjected, her hands still covered in flour. "I'm slaving away in the kitchen. You don't want to miss out!" She winked in Mia's direction.

Jonathan smiled, the laugh lines making parenthesis around his eyes. "Oh, I wish I could stay. But I promised my sister that I'd spend the evening at her house. I can only stay for a drink tonight, but I'd love to have dinner again with all of you sometime soon."

Mia beamed from the inside out.

"Well, a toast then!" Tom encircled the group and raised his cocktail. Everyone followed suit, Zoe and the kids with glasses of sparkling cider, the rest with glasses of red and white wine.

"What are we toasting?" Mia asked.

"I don't know. It's your house." Tom shrugged. "How about to a happy holiday?"

"How about to a new beginning?" Emma chimed in, nudging Mia.

"How about to Paris?" Zoe shouted.

"How about to Mia's new job!" Tom gave a thumbs-up with his free hand.

Jonathan chuckled. "Wow, you guys have a lot to toast." He smiled and slipped his hand around Mia's waist. "This is a group I could get used to."

Mia smiled back and leaned into him. "Hear, hear!" she cheered as they clinked glasses all the way around.

ACKNOWLEDGMENTS

I wrote this book with a deep admiration for Ray Bradbury and a respect for the history of his Los Angeles home. As a Southern California native, familiar with the neighborhood, I wanted to imagine a world where the house wasn't demolished, but instead purchased by an appreciative writer. While my story is fictional, I hope to share a bit of Mr. Bradbury's inspirational spirit with my readers. I'm thankful for his many contributions to the literary community.

To my early readers, Colleen Peterson and Molly Carroll, your feedback to my (sometimes raw) first drafts was invaluable. To my group of cheerleaders, affectionately known as "The Bs," thank you for the encouragement and enthusiasm given along the way. To my sisters, I never take for granted the heaps of support you send my way. A debt of gratitude also goes out to my blog readers at *Have Tote Will Travel.* You allowed me to share another side of my writing, and your loyalty over the years has been much appreciated.

I'd like to thank the people at Sparkpress, Crystal Patriarche, Brooke Warner, and the whole team. I'm grateful to be part of a family of talented authors. Thank you to my copy editor, Valerie Williamson. Barrett Briske, thank you for navigating me through a nerve-wracking permissions process. Julie Metz, you captured everything I wanted in the cover art and then some.

Lastly, a special thank you to my husband, Greg, and kids, Natalie, Lauren, and Ben. I wouldn't have made it this far without your support. Your love means more than all the words.

Justin Earl Photography

NICOLE MEIER is a native Southern Californian who pulled up roots and moved to the Pacific Northwest. She works as a freelance travel and lifestyle writer. She lives in Oregon with her husband and three children. *The House of Bradbury* is her first novel.

ABOUT SPARKPRESS

SparkPress is an independent, hybrid imprint focused on merging the best of the traditional publishing model with new and innovative strategies. We deliver high-quality, entertaining, and engaging content that enhances readers' lives. We are proud to bring to market a list of *New York Times* bestselling, award-winning, and debut authors who represent a wide array of genres, as well as our established, industry-wide reputation for innovative, creative, results-driven success in working with authors. SparkPress, a BookSparks imprint, is a division of SparkPoint Studio, LLC.

Learn more at GoSparkPress.com